An Invitation to Danger

There in the gloom he seemed again to see the face of the frightened girl. His hand holding the weighted hanger stopped halfway down the rack. He could make out the serious, hunted eyes, the thin features, the nervous lips.

She had the key, the password to the hidden world. She knew the answer to the question that dark-engulfed Mackay had been asking.

The imagined lips parted nervously, as if she were about to speak. . . .

FRITZ LEIBER

THE SINFUL ONES

PUBLISHED BY POCKET BOOKS NEW YORK

POCKET BOOKS, a Simon & Schuster division of
GULF & WESTERN CORPORATION
1230 Avenue of the Americas, New York, N.Y. 10020

ISBN: 0-671-83575-0

First Pocket Books printing October, 1980

10 9 8 7 6 5 4 3 2 1

POCKET and colophon are trademarks of Simon & Schuster.

Printed in the U.S.A.

CHAPTER ONE

The Frightened Girl

WHEN CARR MACKEY first caught sight of the frightened girl, he was feeling exceptionally bored. The offices of General Employment seemed a jail, time an unclimbable wall, life a straitjacket, the very air a slow-setting invisible cement. Even thoughts of Marcia failed to put any color in his gray mood.

He had just finished up with an applicant. The empty wire basket on his desk meant that he had nothing to do for a while.

The other interviewers were still busy with their share of the horde of job-seekers who trickled into Chicago's Loop, converged on General Employment, and then went their ways again, as aimlessly as ants trailing into and out of a hole, and as defenseless in the long run against the turn of a giant heel.

Anything was more interesting than people, Carr felt. Yet a glance at the big clock told him it was only three-thirty, and the prospect of an empty hour-and-a-half seemed almost worse than one filled with people, no matter how stupid and lifeless.

It was just then that the frightened girl came into the waiting room. Without looking around she sat down on one of the benches, wooden and high-backed, rather like church pews.

Carr watched her through the huge glass panel that made everything in the waiting room silent and slightly unreal. Just a girl in a cardigan. College type, a bit affected, dark hair falling untidily to her shoulders. And nervous—in fact, frightened. Still, just an ordinary girl. Nothing tremendously intriguing or pretty about her.

And yet . . . it was as if Carr had been sitting for hours in front of a curtain that he had become quite certain would never rise, when suddenly something (who knows what?—a scrape of feet in the orchestra pit, a slight dimming of the light, the sense of an actor peering through one of the eyeholes in the ponderous cloth) made him feel that it might not be too painful to wait a little longer.

"Ow, my feet!"

Carr looked around. Miss Zabel's features were contorted into a simulation of intense pain as she picked up the record cards on his desk.

"Shoes hurt?" he inquired sympathetically.

She nodded. Her topknot of unruly hair bobbed decisively. "You're lucky," she told him. "You can sit at a desk."

"That can be painful too."

She looked at him skeptically and teetered off.

Carr's gaze flipped back to the frightened girl. There had been a change. Whatever she'd been doing—biting her lip, twisting her fingers—she wasn't any longer. She sat quite still, looking straight ahead, arms close to her sides.

Another woman had come into the waiting room. A big blonde, rather handsome in a poster-ish way, with a stunningly perfect hairdo. Yet her tailored suit gave her a mannish look, she had a cruel mouth, and there was something queer about her eyes. Several job-categories jumped into Carr's mind: receptionist, model (a shade heavy for that), buyer, private detective. She stood inside the door, looking around. She saw the frightened girl. She started toward her.

The phone on Carr's desk buzzed.

As he picked it up, he noticed that the big blonde had stopped in front of the frightened girl and was looking down at her. The frightened girl seemed rather pathetically trying to ignore her.

"That you, Carr?" came over the phone.

He felt a rush of pleasure. Odd, what the mere sound of a desired woman's voice will do to you, when all your thoughts about her have left you cold.

"Oh, hello, Marcia dear," he said quickly.

"Darling, Keaton's given me some more details on the new business he's planning. I think it's a really sharp idea. And he's all set to go ahead."

"It did sound rather clever from the bit you told me," Carr said cautiously, his first warmth a bit dashed. As he searched his mind for the best way to put Marcia off, his gaze went idly back to the little drama beyond the glass wall. The big blonde had sat herself down beside the

6

frightened girl and had taken her hand, seemed to be stroking it. The frightened girl was still staring straight ahead—desperately, Carr thought.

"And so of course I told Keaton about you. Darling, he's very interested. He definitely wants to see you some time this week. It means a real job for you, Carr."

Carr felt a not unfamiliar sag of dismay. "But Marcia . . ."

The fast, confident voice cut him off. "We'll talk it over tonight. It's really a marvelous chance. Goodbye, darling."

He heard a click. He put back the phone and prepared to feel depressed as well as bored—God, if Marcia would only stop trying to make a success of him—a job for the job-purveyor, what a laugh!—when a flurry of footsteps made him look up.

The frightened girl was approaching his desk.

The big blonde had followed her as far as the door in the glass wall and was watching her from it.

The frightened girl sat down in the applicant's chair. She half turned toward Carr, but she didn't look him in the eye. She gathered her wool jacket at the throat in a way that struck Carr as almost comically melodramatic, as if she were about to say, "I'm half frozen," or "They wouldn't hang me . . . would they?" or "Darling, your hands—I'm afraid of them," or just "My God! Gas!"

Right there Carr got the feeling, "It's started." Though he hadn't the faintest idea what had started. The big curtain hadn't lifted an inch, but someone had darted out in front of it.

Another part of his mind was thinking that this was merely a rather odd applicant—as how many of them weren't?—and he'd better get busy with her.

He twitched her a smile. "I don't believe I have your application blank yet, Miss . . . ?"

The frightened girl did not answer.

To put her at ease, Carr rattled on, "Not that it matters. We can talk things over while we wait for the clerk to bring it."

Still she didn't look at him.

"I suppose you did fill out an application blank and that you were sent to me?" he added, a bit sharply.

Then he saw that she was trembling and he became aware of a hush that had nothing whatever to do

7

with ordinary noises. There still came the rat-ta-ta-tat of typing, the murmur of conversation from the applicant-interviewer pairs at the other desks, the click of slides from the curtained cubicle where someone was getting an eye-test—all the usual small sounds of General Employment. And behind them Chicago's unceasing mutter, rising and falling with the passing El trains.

But the other silence continued. Even the resounding click of the big minute clock on the wall, that sometimes caught Carr up with a jerk, did not break it.

It was as if those sounds—the whole office—Chicago—everything—had become mere lifeless background for a chalk-faced girl in a sloppy cardigan, arms huddled tight around her, hands gripping her thin elbows, staring at him horror-struck.

For some incredible reason, she seemed to be frightened of *him*.

She shrank down in the chair, her white-circled eyes fixed on his. As his gaze followed her movements, another shudder went through her. The tip of her tongue licked her upper lip. Then she said in a small, terrified voice, "All right, you've got me. But don't draw it out. Don't play with me. Get it over with."

Carr checked the impulse to grimace incredulously. He chuckled and said, "I know how you feel. Coming into a big employment office does seem an awful plunge. But we won't chain you to a rivet gun," he went on, with a wild attempt at humor, "or send you to Buenos Aires. It's still a free country."

She did not react. Carr looked away uneasily. The queer hush was eating at his nerves—a dizzy, tight-skinned feeling, as if he were coming down with a chill. He groped for the change in his mood. He knew there had been one, but it was so all-embracing that he couldn't put his finger on it. The big names on the maps are always the hardest to find.

The blonde was still watching from the doorway, her manner implying that she owned the place, or any other she might stalk into. Her eyes looked whiter than they should be and they didn't seem quite to focus, although that didn't diminish, but rather intensified, the impression of hungry, hostile peering.

He looked back at the frightened girl. Her hands still gripped her elbows, but she was leaning forward now and studying his face, as if everything in the world depended on what she saw there.

"You're not one of them?"

He frowned puzzledly. "Them? Who?"

"You're not?" she repeated, still watching his face.

"I don't understand," he said.

"Don't you know what you are?" she asked with a sudden fierceness. "Don't you know whether you're one of them or not?"

"I don't know what you're talking about," he assured her, "and I haven't the faintest idea of whom you mean by 'them.'"

Slowly her hands loosened their hold on her elbows and trailed into her lap. "No," she said, "I guess you're not. You haven't their filthy look. But then . . ." her lips twitched, ". . . I must have been fated to come here at this exact moment. And say just these words. Oh, what a crazy, crazy joke." She was trembling again. "Or else you really are. . . ?" and there came into her eyes an important, but quite incomprehensible question.

"Look," Carr said gently, "you'd better explain things from the beginning. Just what . . ."

"Please, not now," she begged unevenly.

Carr realized suddenly that her shaking was that of repressed hysteria and that she was asking for time to get herself under control.

He looked away, trying to fathom his reactions. By all rights he should type this girl as belonging to the lunatic fringe of unemployables that clutter up every employment office. Probably her application blank, if she'd filled one out, was being held up because Miss Zabel or one of the other girls had noticed some weird discrepancies in it. He should be thinking of a smooth way to terminate the interview and ease her out.

But instead his mind was searching for a more logical pattern than psychosis underlying her actions, as if convinced that such a pattern existed and he must discover it.

All at once the smudge on her left hand, the intellectual pursing of her features, the uneasy hunch of her shoulders, and the long, irregular curves in which her brown hair fell to them, seemed to suggest a thousand things.

Somehow he had become involved.

Love? That might do in a romantic novel. Here some vastly more plausible explanation was required.

9

A sense of lifelessness in his surroundings continued to oppress him, had even deepened. Somewhere in the past few minutes he had crossed the boundary that separates the ordinary from the extraordinary, from more than the extraordinary. But how could he know, when there was not one iota of concrete evidence and he had only intuition to back him up?

"Who's that woman following you?" he asked her quietly. "Is she one of 'them?' "

The terror returned to her face. "I can't tell you that. Please don't ask me. And please don't look at her. It's terribly important that she doesn't think I've seen her."

"But how could she possibly think otherwise after the way she planked herself down beside you?"

"Please, oh please!" She was almost whimpering. "I can't tell you why. It's just terribly important that we act naturally, that we seem to be doing whatever it is that we're supposed to be doing. Can we?"

Carr studied her. She was obviously close to actual hysteria. "Sure," he said. He leaned back in his chair, smiled at her, and raised his voice a trifle. "Just what sort of job do you feel would make the best use of your abilities, Miss. . . ?"

"Job? Oh yes, that's why I'd have come here, isn't it?" For a moment she stared at him helplessly. Then, hurriedly, the words tumbling over each other, she began to talk. "Let's see, I can play the piano. Not very well. Mostly classical. I've studied it a lot, though. I once wanted to be a concert pianist. And I've done some amateur acting. And I can read books very fast. Fiction, that is. I know my way around libraries pretty well. And I used to play a mediocre game of tennis—" Her grotesquely animated expression froze. "But that isn't at all the sort of thing you want to know, is it?"

Carr shrugged. "Helps give me a picture. Did some amateur acting once, in college." He kept his voice casual. "Have you had any regular jobs?"

"I once read books for a publisher. Just fiction, though. And for a little while I worked in an architect's office."

"Did you learn to read blueprints?" he asked.

"Blueprints?" The girl shivered. "Not much, I'm afraid. I hate patterns of all sorts, unless they're so mixed up that no one but myself knows they're patterns. Patterns are traps. Once you start living according to a pattern, other people know how to get control of you." She leaned forward confidingly, her fingers hooking onto the edge of the desk. "Oh, and I'm a good judge of people. I have to be. I suppose you have to be too." The incomprehensible question came back into her eyes. "Don't you really know what you are?" she asked softly. "Haven't you found out yet? Why, you must be almost forty. Surely in that time . . . Oh, you must know."

"I still haven't the ghost of an idea of what you're talking about," said Carr. "What am I?"

The girl hesitated.

"Tell me," he said.

She shook her head. "If you honestly don't know, I'm not sure I should tell you. As long as you don't know, you're safe. Relatively safe, that is. If I had had the opportunity of not knowing, I know how I would have chosen. As least I know how I'd choose now. Oh God, yes."

Carr began to feel like the anecdotal man to whom a beautiful woman hands a note written in French which no one will translate for him. "Please stop being mysterious," he said. "Just what is it about me that's so important? Something I don't know about my background? Or about my race? My political leanings? My psychological type? My love life?"

"But if you don't know," she went on, disregarding his questions, "and if I don't tell you, then I'm letting you run a blind risk. Not a big one, but very terrible. And with them so close and perhaps suspecting . . . Oh, it's so hard to decide."

"They're killing me!"

Carr jerked around. Miss Zabel squinted at him in agony, dropped an application folder in the wire basket, and hobbled off. Carr looked at the folder. It wasn't for a girl at all. It started, "Jimmie Kozacs. Male. Age 43."

He became aware that the frightened girl was studying his face again, as if she saw something there that she had missed the first time. It seemed to cause her dismay.

"Maybe you never were, until today," she said, more to herself than him. "That would explain your not knowing. Maybe my bursting in here was what did it. Maybe I was the one who awakened you."

She clenched her hands, torturing the palms with the long, untapered fingers, and Carr's sardonic remark about having been awakened quite early in life died before it

11

was born. "To think that I would ever do that to any-one!" she continued. "To think that I would ever cause anyone the agony that *he* caused me! Oh, if only there were someone I could talk to, someone who could tell me what to do."

The bleak misery in her voice caught at Carr. "What *is* the matter?" he pleaded. "Please tell me."

The girl looked shocked. "Now?" Her glance half-circled the room, strayed toward the glass wall. "No, not here. I can't." The fingers of her right hand rippled as if they were playing a frantic arpeggio. Suddenly they dived into the pocket of her cardigan and came out with a stubby, chewed pencil. She ripped a sheet from Carr's scratch pad and began to scribble hurriedly.

As Carr watched her doubtfully, a big area of gray cloth swam into view. It was Tom Elvested, come ambling over from the next desk. The girl gave Tom a quick, queer look, then went on scribbling. Tom ignored her.

"Say, Carr," he began amiably, "Midge and I are go-ing on a date tonight. She's got a girl-friend I think you'd like. A swell kid, lot of brains, but sort of shy and retir-ing. We'd like you to come along with us."

"Sorry, I can't, I've got a date," Carr told him irritably. It annoyed him that Tom should discuss personal matters in front of an applicant.

"Now, don't get the idea I'm asking you to do social service work," Tom went on, a little huffily. "This girl's darn good-looking and a lot more your type than—" he broke off.

"Than Marcia, were you going to say?" Carr asked him. "At any rate it's Marcia I've got a date with."

Tom looked at Carr for a moment. Then, "Okay," he said, fading back. "Sorry you can't come."

The frightened girl was still scribbling. The scratch of her pencil seemed to Carr the only real sound in the whole office. He glanced guardedly down the aisle. The big blonde with the queer eyes was still at the door, but she had moved ungraciously aside to make way for a dumpy man in blue jeans, who was looking around un-certainly.

The dumpy man veered toward Miss Zabel. Her top-knot bobbed up from her typewriter and she said some-thing. His uncertainty vanished. He gave her an "I getcha, pal" nod and headed for Carr's desk.

The frightened girl noticed him coming, shoved aside paper and pencil in a flurry of haste, and stood up.

"Sit down," said Carr. "That fellow can wait. Incidentally, do you know Tom Elvested?" She disregarded the question and quickly moved into the aisle.

Carr followed her. "I really want to talk with you," he said.

"No," she breathed, edging away from him.

"But we haven't got anywhere yet," he objected.

Suddenly she smiled like a toothpaste ad. "Thank you for being so helpful," she said in a loud voice. "I'll think over what you've told me, though I don't think the job is one which would appeal to me." She poked out her hand. Automatically he took it. It was icy.

"Don't follow me," she whispered. "And if you care the least bit for me or my safety, don't do anything, whatever happens."

"But I don't even know your name . . ." His voice trailed off. She was striding rapidly down the aisle. The big blonde was standing squarely in her path. The girl did not swerve an inch. Then, just as they were about to collide, the other woman lifted her hand and gave the girl a stinging slap across the cheek.

Carr started, winced, took a forward step, froze.

The other woman stepped aside, smiling sardonically.

The girl rocked, wavered for a step or two, then walked on without turning her head.

No one said anything, no one did anything, no one jumped up, no one even looked up, at least not conspicuously, although everyone in the office must have heard the slap if they hadn't seen it. But with the universal middle-class reluctance, Carr thought, to get mixed up in any trouble unless they were forced to, they pretended not to notice.

The big blonde flicked into place a shellacked curl, glancing around her as if at so much dirt. Leisurely she turned and stalked out.

Carr walked back to his desk. His face felt hot, his mind was turbulent. The office around him seemed out of key, turbidly sinister, a little like the scenery of a nightmare—the downtown gloom pressing on the tall, faintly grimed windows, the hazy highlights on the polished desks, the meaningless phrases hanging in the air.

The dumpy man in blue jeans had already taken the girl's place, but for the moment Carr ignored him. He didn't sit down. The scrap of paper on which the girl had scribbled caught his eye. He picked it up.

Watch out (it read) for the wall-eyed blonde, the young man without a hand, and the affable-seeming older man. But the small dark man with glasses is your friend.

Carr frowned grotesquely. "Wall-eyed blonde . . ." — that must be the woman who had been watching. But as for the other three —"small dark man with glasses is your friend . . ."—it sounded like a charade.

"Thanks, I guess I will," said the dumpy man casually, plucking at something in the air.

Carr started to turn over the paper to see if she'd scribbled anything on the opposite side, when—

"No, I got a light," said the dumpy man.

Carr looked at him and forgot everything else. The dumpy man had lit a match and was cupping it about three inches from his curiously puckered lips. There was a slight hissing noise and the flame curtsied as he sucked in. He smiled gratefully over his cupped hands at Carr's empty chair. Then one hand shook out the match and the other moved in toward his lips, paused a moment, then moved out about a foot from his face, first and second fingers extended like a priest giving a blessing. After an interval the hand moved in again, the hissing inhalation was repeated, and the dumpy man threw back his head and exhaled through tightened nostrils.

Obviously the man was smoking a cigarette.

Only there was no cigarette.

Carr wanted to laugh, there was something so droll about the realism of the movements. He remembered the pantomimes in the acting class at college. You pretended to drive an automobile or eat a dinner or write a letter, without any props, just going through the motions. In that class the dumpy man would have rated an A-plus.

"Yeah, that's right," the dumpy man said to Carr's empty chair, wagging his extended fingers over the brown-gummed ashtray.

Suddenly Carr didn't want to laugh at all. Obviously, as obviously as any such things can be, this man wasn't an actor.

"Yeah, I did it about eight months. Came into it from weld assembly," continued the dumpy man between im-

14

aginary puffs. "I was coming up from my second test when me and the wife decided to move here to get away from her mother."

Carr felt a qualm of uneasiness. He hesitated, then slowly bent forward from where he was standing, until his face was hardly a foot from that of the dumpy man and almost squarely in front of it.

The dumpy man didn't react, didn't seem to see him at all, kept talking through him to the chair.

"Oh, it's dirty work all right. I had my share of skin trouble. But I can take it."

"Stop it," said Carr.

"No, I passed it after I'd been there three months." The dumpy man was amiably emphatic. "It was my full inspector's I was coming up for. I was due to get my stamps."

Carr shivered. "Stop it," he said very distinctly. "Stop it."

"Sure, all sorts of stuff. Circular and longitudinal magnetism. Machine parts, forging, welds, tie-beams . . ."

"Stop it," Carr repeated and grabbed him firmly by the shoulder.

What happened made Carr wish he hadn't. The dumpy man's face grew strained and red, like an enraged baby's. An intense throbbing was transmitted to Carr's hand. And from the lips came a mounting, meaningless mutter.

Carr jerked back. He felt craven and weak, as helpless as a child. He edged away until he was standing behind Tom Elvested, who was engrossed with a client.

He could hardly bring his voice up to a whisper.

"Tom, I've got a man who's acting funny. Would you help me?"

Tom didn't look up, apparently didn't hear.

Across the room Carr saw a gray-mustached man walking briskly. He hurried over to him, looking back apprehensively at the dumpy man, who was still sitting there red-faced.

"Dr. Wexler," he blurted, "I've got a lunatic on my hands and I think he's about to throw a fit. Would you—?"

But Dr. Wexler walked on without slackening his pace and disappeared through the black curtains of the eye-testing cubicle.

At that instant, as Carr watched the black curtains swing together, a sudden spasm of extreme terror seized

15

him. As if something huge and hostile were poised behind him, he dared not lift his head, look up, make a move.

It was like the momentary chill he had felt when no one had reacted to the slap. Only much more intense.

His feelings were a little like those of a man in a waxworks museum, who speaks to a guide only to find that he has addressed one of the wax figures.

His paralyzed thoughts, suddenly working like lightning, snatched at the analogy and worried it morbidly.

What if the whole world were like a waxworks museum? In motion, of course, like clockworks, but utterly mindless, purposeless, mechanical. What if he, a wax figure like the others, had suddenly come alive and stepped out of his place, and the whole show was going on without him, because it was just a machine and didn't care or know whether he was there or not?

That would explain the dumpy man going through the motions of an interview—one mechanical toy-figure carrying on just as well without its partner. It would explain why Tom and Dr. Wexler had disregarded him.

What if it really were true?

What if the ends of the earth were nearer to you than the mind you thought lay behind the face you spoke to?

What if the things people said, the things that seemed to mean so much, were something recorded on a kind of phonograph record a million years ago?

What if you were all alone?

For an instant longer his thought-train—it had taken only a few moments—held him paralyzed. Then he came to himself with a start.

Life flooded back into the office. People moved and spoke. He almost laughed out loud at his ridiculous spasm of terror.

Why, what an idiot he'd been to get alarmed because Tom, who doubtless felt huffy toward him because of their last conversation, had momentarily ignored a mumbled, perhaps unheard, question? Or because the same thing had happened with Dr. Wexler, whose deafness and preoccupation were both notorious!

And how silly of him to lose his nerve just because he had got an applicant who was something of a psychotic!

He straightened himself and walked back to his desk, warily, but with self-confidence.

The dumpy man was still muttering at the air, but his face had assumed its original color. He didn't look violent.

16

Carr disregarded him and glanced at the application blank Miss Zabel had brought a few minutes earlier: "Jimmie Kozacs. Age 43."

The dumpy man looked about that age.

A little farther down the blank, his eye caught the words, "Magnetic Inspector." If he remembered rightly the duties of the job in question, they fitted with the things the dumpy man had been saying.

The dumpy man got up. Again he plucked something from the air. "So all I got to do is show 'em this at the gate?" he remarked gravely. "Thanks a lot, er . . ." He glanced at the nameplate on Carr's desk. ". . . Mr. Mackay. Aw, don't get up. Well, thanks a lot."

Heartily the dumpy man shook hands with nothing, turned and walked off. Carr watched him go. A smile that was half nervous amusement, half relief, flickered around his lips.

Miss Zabel came limping by with a stack of file-folders.

"I swear I'm going to cut them off and donate them to medical research," she moaned to Carr.

Carr chortled. His sense of normalcy was restored.

CHAPTER TWO

The Stopped Clock

CARR TOOK THE brass-edged steps three at a time, crossed the lobby, pushed hurriedly through the revolving door which always made him feel like a squirrel in a wheel. He joined the crowd streaming toward Michigan Boulevard.

Street lights were beginning to supplement the canyoned twilight. Newsboys were shouting. Bus stops and islands of dubious safety were crowded, likewise the stairways leading to the long El platforms. From the wide doorways of multi-story garages, cars were edging forward by stages, bluffing their way into the thick traffic. Other cars were being honked at while they paused to pick up riders. Lone pedestrains darted between bumpers in a way that would have made everyone flinch in a less punch-drunk city than Chicago.

It was wonderful to lose yourself in the rush-hour rhythm, Carr felt, to get away from General Employment, and to be where people were people, not just an assortment of job capacities, salary levels, and letters of reference. Of course Marcia was going to revive that distressing job question, apply it to him directly—but not for a couple of hours, thank God!

Preoccupation with people considered solely as clients of General Employment must be what was wrong with him, Carr decided. That must be the explanation of his fit of nerves this afternoon. For so long he had thought of people as mere human raw material, as just something that went with application blanks and it would be a lot more convenient if they were shipped in boxes—for so long had this attitude been pounded into him, month after boring month, that now people were having their revenge on him, by acting woodenly toward him, as if he didn't exist.

Carr chuckled. The dumpy man's psychosis had been an odd one. He'd read about cases where insane people perform some action over and over again, meaninglessly —even up to complicated dramatic interludes, complete with words and gestures. But you'd think such interludes would revolve around some situation of greater tragic potentialities than merely applying for a job.

Still, when you came to think of it, what situation has greater tragic potentialities than the attempt to get a job?

He reached Michigan Boulevard. The wall of empty space on the other side, fronting the wall of buildings on this, gave a lift to his spirits. A fringe of restless trees hinted at the lake beyond. The Art Institute traced a classic pattern against the stone-gray sky. Here the air still seemed to carry a trace of freshness from this morning's rain. As he turned north, stepping out briskly, he began to think of Marcia, but after a bit his attention was diverted to a small man walking a little way ahead of him at an equally fast pace.

Carr's legs were considerably longer, but the small man had a peculiar skip to his stride. His movements gave the impression of elusiveness; he was constantly weaving, seeking the open channels in the crowd. His dark hair was long and untidy.

Carr felt one of those surges of curiosity that an unknown figure sometimes evokes. He was tempted to increase his pace so that he could get a look at the stranger's face.

At that moment the small man whirled around. Carr stopped. The small man peered at him through horn-rimmed, thick-lensed glasses. Then what seemed to be an expression of extreme horror crossed the stranger's face. For a moment he crouched as if paralyzed. Then, all in a rush, he turned and darted away, dancing past people, scurrying from side to side, finally whisking out of sight around the next corner, like a puppet jerked offstage.

Carr felt like laughing wildly. The frightened girl had written, "But the small dark man with glasses is your friend." He certainly hadn't acted that way!

Someone bumped into Carr from behind and he darted forward—half nervous reaction, half belated intention to pursue the small dark man. But after a dozen or so hurtling paces it occurred to him that he was making himself look ridiculous, and in any case he could hardly overcome the fellow's head-start.

It was as if the governor of a machine, temporarily out of order, had begun to function again. He fell back into his former not conspicuously rapid gait. He was back in the rush-hour rhythm.

He looked down the next cross-street. The small dark man was nowhere in sight. He might very well be three blocks away by now, the way he'd been going.

Carr smiled. It occurred to him that he really had no good reason to believe that this was the frightened girl's small dark man. After all—arresting thought!—there must be thousands, tens of thousands of small dark men with glasses in the world.

But he found he couldn't laugh off the incident quite that easily. It had reawakened the same mood that the frightened girl had evoked in him this afternoon—a mood of uneasiness and frustrated excitement. Carr's memory kept picturing the face of the frightened girl.

He pictured her as a college girl, the sort who would cut classes in order to sit on the brink of a fountain and argue very seriously with some young man about the meaning of art. With pencil smudges on her cheeks. The picture fitted, all right. Only consider the howling naivete of her wondering whether she had "awakened" him.

And yet even that question might cut a lot deeper than you'd think. Wasn't there a sense in which he actually was "unawakened?"—a person who'd dodged life, who'd never been truly comfortable with any job or any woman—except Marcia, he reminded himself hurriedly. He'd always had that sense of a vastly richer and more vivid existence just out of reach.

For that matter, didn't most people live their lives without ever really "awakening"—as dull as worms, as mechanical as insects, their thoughts spoon-fed to them by newspaper and radio? Couldn't robots perform the much over-rated "business of living" just as well?

Certainly this afternoon's events had been of a sort to disturb the imagination most peculiarly. He couldn't offhand think of a single satisfactory explanation for the frightened girl's actions: insanity, neurosis, or some actual danger. Or perhaps just a joke?

No, there'd been something undeniably sinister about the wall-eyed blonde, and something in her attitude toward the frightened girl suggestive of a morbid spiritual tyranny. Carr flushed, remembering the slap.

And then those encounters with the dumpy man and the small dark man coming so pat, the latter just as predicted. Carr had the uneasy conviction that he had blundered somehow into a vast shadowy web.

He had reached the Michigan Avenue bridge. In the dusk the Chicago River was a dark, matte floor. He could sense the fine sprinkling of soot that filmed the ripples.

He noticed an old black motor-barge approaching the bridge. A small, clumsy looking vessel with a long low cabin and a squat stack.

But it was the bargeman who was most impressive. He was a man of gigantic stature, big-framed. His face was big-jawed, deep-eyed, a fighter's, but above it rose a great white forehead. His clothes were rough and black, yet Carr fancied that there was about him an air of intellectual power. In his right hand, like a pike, he carried a wicked-looking boathook with a thick shaft almost twice as long as himself.

As the barge nerared the bridge he slowly lifted his head and fixed on Carr a gaze so intense, so speculative, so meaningful, that Carr almost jerked back from the rail.

He was still looking at Carr, his face a half-squared white oval against the black of his garments and the deck, as the barge floated on under the bridge.

All the way home, over the big windy bridge, between the gleaming white and yellow-gray pylons of the Wrigley Building and the Tribune Tower, through the dark, gay

20

streets of the near North Side and up to the very steps of the old brownstone house in which he rented a room, Carr tried to discern the outlines of the web in which he seemed to have become entangled. He was quite unsuccessful, and as for a spider, there was not even the shadow of one. What possible linkage could there be between a frightened girl, an unbalanced magnetic inspector, a stranger who fled at sight of you, and perhaps a gargantuan bargeman?

The hallway was musty and dim. He felt in his pigeonhole, but there was no mail. He hurried up the ornately balustraded stairs, relic of the opulent days of the 1890's. On the stairs it was darker. A small stained-glass window, mostly patches of dark red and purple, gave the only light.

Just as he reached the turn, he thought he saw himself coming toward himself in the gloom.

The illusion lasted only a moment. Then he recognized the figure for his reflection in the huge mirror, misty, time-streaked and speckled, that occupied most of the wall space of the landing. It had happened to him before.

But still he stood there, staring at the dark-engulfed image of a tall, rather slightly-built man with light hair and small, regular features. A trivial experience had taken on a new meaning, had caused a crystallization of emotion and thought.

There he was—Carr Mackay. And all around him was an unknown universe. And just what, in that universe, did Carr Mackay mean or matter? What was the real significance of the routine, the dark rhythm, that was rushing him through life at an ever-hastening pace toward a grave somewhere? Did it have any significance—that is, any significance a man could accept or endure—especially when any break in the rhythm, like this afternoon's events, could make it seem so dead and purposeless, an endless marching and counter-marching of marionettes?

He ran blindly past the reflection up the stairs.

In the hall above it was darker still. A bulb had burned out and not been replaced. He felt his way down the corridor and opened the door of his own room.

It was high-ceilinged and comfortable, with rich old woodwork that countless layers of cheap paint couldn't quite obliterate, and there was an old brass bed with rods and knobs like a fancy birdcage. Starting in at once to change his clothes, Carr tried to let the place take him and cradle him in its suggestion of the familiar and of his life with Marcia and her crowd, make him forget that lost Carr Mackay down there in the mirror. There were his golf clubs in the corner, the books on sailing, the case of poker chips on the mantlepiece, the box for shirt studs with the theater program beside it, and the sleek military hairbrushes Marcia had given him. But tonight they seemed as arbitrary and poignantly useless an assortment of objects as those placed in an old Egyptian grave, to accompany their owner on his long trek through the underworld.

They were not as alive, even, as the two dusty books on metaphysics he had bought in college and never waded more than a quarter through, or the little plaster plaque of the masks of comedy and tragedy presented fifteen years ago to the members of the college dramatic association, or the long-unopened box of chessmen, or the tarnished silver half-pint flask.

He slung his brown suit on a hanger, took it in the closet, and reached down his blue suit, still in its wrapper from the cleaner's.

There in the gloom he seemed again to see the face of the frightened girl. His hand holding the weighted hanger stopped halfway down from the rack. He could make out the serious, hunted eyes, the thin features, the nervous lips.

She had the key, the password to the hidden world. She knew the answer to the question that dark-engulfed Mackay had been asking.

The imagined lips parted nervously, as if she were about to speak.

With an angry exhalation of held breath, Carr jerked back into the room. What could he be thinking? It was only in wistful, half-baked books that men of thirty-nine fell in love with moody, mysterious, coltish college girls. Or were caught up in glamorously sinister intrigues that existed solely in such girls' hot-house brains.

He put on his blue suit, then started to transfer to it the stuff in the pockets of the brown one. He came upon the note the frightened girl had scribbled. He must have shoved it into his pocket when the dumpy man had started misbehaving. He turned it over and saw that he hadn't read all of it.

If you want to meet me again in spite of dangers, I'll be by the lion's tail near the five sisters tonight at eight.

His lips twisted in a wry, incredulous smile. Then he spat out a laugh. That tore it! If that didn't prove she'd been suckled on *The Prisoner of Zenda* and weaned on *Graustark*, he'd like to know. Lion's tail and five sisters! She probably carried the Rajah's ruby in a bag around her neck and wrote love letters with a black swan's quill. In short, she went in for a brand of melodrama and high mystification that had gone out with the bustle. Here was the key to her antics, and she could stop haunting his imagination right now.

Why, there was no question but that Marcia was the right woman for him, even if at times she was a little too eager to change his life. Capable, charming, successful, mature. An executive with an important publishing firm. Competent at both business and pleasure. His kind. Sailed and golfed with him and the crowd, played a shrewd game of poker, went to theaters and interesting parties, knew important people. He and Marcia would reach some satisfying understanding soon, maybe even get married. What competition could be offered by a mere maladjusted girl?

"But," something reminded him quietly, "didn't you decide at the office that it wasn't anything like love that was the bond between you and the frightened girl? Aren't you trying to dodge the problem by shifting it to an entirely different emotional level?"

He hurried into the bathroom, rubbing his chin. Marcia liked him to be well-groomed and his beard felt pretty conspicuous. He looked into the mirror to confirm his suspicions and once again he saw a different Carr Mackay.

The one down there on the stairs had seemed lost. This one, framed in surgical white, looked trapped. A neat, wooden little Mackay who went trudging through life without inquiring what any of the signposts meant, who always grabbed at pleasures he didn't want, who kept selling himself this, that, and the other thing—customer Jekyll and salesman Hyde. A stupid Mackay, who always stuck to the ordained routine. A dummy.

He really ought to shave, yes, but the way he was feeling, the sooner he and Marcia got started drinking, the better. He'd skip shaving this once.

23

As he made this decision, he was conscious of a dispro-portionate feeling of guilt.

But everyone, at some time or another, finds himself at-taching grotesque importance to some trivial action. Like stepping on, or not stepping on, a crack in the sidewalk.

He'd probably been reading too many "Five O'Clock Shadow" ads.

Forget it.

He hurried into the rest of his clothes, started toward the door, stopped by the bureau, pulled open the top drawer, looked for a moment as the three flat pints of whiskey nestling inside it. Then he shut the drawer quickly and hurried into the hall, down the stairs, averting his eyes from the mirror, passed quickly through the still shadowy hall, and out into the street.

It was a relief to know he'd be with Marcia in a few minutes. But eight dark blocks are eight dark blocks, and they have to be walked, and to walk them takes time no matter how rapidly you stride. Time for your sense of purpose and security to dwindle to nothing. Time for the familiar to become the chillingly unfamiliar. Time for the patterns you live by to lose their neat outlines. Time to get away from the ads and the pink lights and the television voices and to think a little bit about the universe—to real-ize that it's a place of mystification and death, with no more feeling than a sausage grinder for the life oozing through it.

The buildings to either side became the walls of a black runway, and the occasional passers-by, shadow-swathed automatons.

He became conscious of the dark rhythm of existence as a nerve-twisting, insistent thing that tugged at him like a marionette's strings, trying to drag him back to some pattern from which he had departed. A compound of hurrying footsteps, roaring engines, screeching streetcars, drumming propellers, surging oceans, spinning planets, plunging stars, and still something more.

Just a mood, he told himself, a very intense mood. But wasn't that saying enough? Wasn't the essence of a mood one's inability to combat it? And the more intelligent you were, the more readily you could see through all dodges and rationalizations back to the cold, harsh, unfathomable reality of the mood itself.

Being with Marcia would fix him up, he told himself, as the dark facades crept slowly by. She at least couldn't ever become a stranger. There was too much between them. Once with her, he would snap back to normal.

But he had forgotten her face.

A trivial thing. It is always easy momentairly to forget a face, no matter how familiar. Like a name, or the place where you've put something for safe-keeping. And the more you try to remember it, the more the precise details elude you.

Carr tried. A hundred faces blinked and faded in his mind, some hauntingly suggestive of Marcia, some grotesquely dissimilar. Girls he had known in college, job aplicants of months ago whom he had never thought of since, pictures in magazines, faces glimpsed for a moment in a crowded street, others with no source-tag at all.

Light from a first-story window spilled on the face of a girl in a blue slicker just as she passed him. His heart pounded as he walked on. He had almost grabbed her and said, "Marcia!" And she hadn't been Marcia's type at all.

He walked faster. The apartment tower where Marcia lived edged into view, grew threateningly tall.

He hurried up the flagstone walk flanked by shrubbery. The lobby was a long useless room furnished in some supposedly Spanish style, with lots of carved wood and red leather. He stopped at the desk. The clerk was at the back of the cubicle, talking to someone over the phone. Carr waited, but the clerk seemed determined to prolong the conversation. Carr cleared his throat. The clerk yawned and languorously flexed the arm that held the receiver, as if to call attention to the gold seal-ring and cuff-linked wrist.

The automatic elevator was waiting, the door open, the cage dark. Carr delayed no longer. He stepped in and pushed the seven button.

Nothing happened.

After jabbing the button a couple of more times, he decided he'd better tell the clerk it was out of order.

But just then the door closed, the light blinked on, and the cage started upward.

It was a small cage. Vermillion panels, brass fittings, a carpet of darker red. A small placard said that it could safely carry 1,500 pounds. The vermillion was darkened where people had leaned, and worn spots showed where packages had been rested on the brass rail and things stuck behind it.

The cage stopped at seven. The door opened. A fat man in a thick overcoat took his finger off the outside button and stepped inside without waiting. Carr squeezed past his paunch, turned around as soon as he was through the door and snapped, "I beg your pardon!" But the door was already closing and the boorish fat man made no rejoinder.

Carr walked down the red-carpeted hall. In front of Marcia's door he hesitated. She mightn't like him barging in this way. But who could be expected always to wait the pleasure of that prissy clerk?

Behind him he heard the cage stop at the ground floor. He noticed that the door he faced was ajar.

He pushed it open a few inches.

"Marcia," he called. "Marcia?" His voice came out huskily.

He stepped inside, into the living room. The reading lamp with its white, tufted shade showed dull pearl walls, white bookcase, blue over-stuffed sofa with a coat and yellow silk scarf tossed across it. and a faint curl of cigarette smoke from somewhere.

Marcia wouldn't go off and leave the door like that.

The bedroom door was open. He corssed to it, his footsteps soundless on the thick carpet. He stopped.

Marcia was sitting on an upholstered stool before a big-mirrored dressing table. Over a chair to one side a gray silk dressing gown was thrown. She was wearing absolutely nothing. A squashed cigarette was smoldering in a tiny silver ash tray. She was lacquering her nails.

That was all. But to Carr it seemed that he had blundered into one of those elaborately realistic department store window displays. He almost expected to see faces peering in the dark window, seven stories up.

Modern bedroom in rose and smoke. Seated mannequin at vanity table. Perhaps a placard, party in script: "Point up your Pinks with Gray."

He stood there stupidly, a step short of the doorway, saying nothing, making no move.

In the mirror her eyes seemed to meet his. He couldn't believe that she was unaware of his presence. He had never known her so brazenly immodest.

She went on lacquering her nails.

She might be angry with him for coming up without the obligatory phone call. But it wasn't like Marcia to choose this queer way of showing her displeasure—and herself.

Or was it? Was she deliberately trying to tease him?

He watched her face in the mirror. It was the one he had forgotten, all right. There were the firm lips, the cool forehead framed by reddish hair, the fleeting quirks of expression—not the ones he was most used to, but definitely hers.

Yet recognition did not bring the sense of absolute certainty it should. Something was lacking—the feeling of a reality behind the face, animating it.

She finished her nails and held them out to dry.

A sharp surge of uneasiness went through Carr. This was nonsensical, he told himself. He must move or speak.

She sat more erect and drew back her shoulders. A faint, admiring and self-satisfied smile settled into her lips. With the pads of her fingertips, still being careful about the polish, she lightly stroked her breasts—upward, almost unnecessarily. Her smile grew dreamy.

The finger-pads closed in on the aureoles and pinched the small nipples. He thought he could see them stiffen.

He felt himself stiffen.

His throat was constricted and his legs felt numb. And looking at her, tauntingly nude, teasingly erotic, he took a forward step. She had no right to tempt him so—

And then all of a sudden it came back: the awful feeling he'd had that afternoon. It stopped him in his tracks.

What if Marcia weren't really alive at all, not consciously alive, but just part of the dance of mindless atoms, a clockworks show that included the whole world, except himself? Merely by coming a few minutes ahead of time, merely by omitting to shave, he had broken the clockwork rhythm. That was why the clerk hadn't spoken to him, that was why the elevator hadn't worked when he'd first pushed the button, that was why the fat man had ignored him, that was why Marcia didn't greet him. It wasn't *time* yet for those little acts in the clockworks show.

The creamy telephone tinkled. Lifting it gingerly, fingers stiffly spread, the figure at the vanity held it to her ear a moment and said, "Certainly. Send him up."

She inspected her nails, waved them, regarded her reflection in the glass, reached for the gray negligee, and—her smile at herself in the mirror became mischievous and (there was the suggestion of a conspiratorial wink) a touch cruel. She drew back her hand, crossed it over the other across her knees, and sat there primly upright, "marking time." But her smile continued to dance.

27

Through the open door Carr could hear the drone of the rising cage.

The cage stopped. There was the soft jolt of its automatic door opening. Carr waited for footsteps. They didn't come.

That was *his* elevator, he thought with a shudder, the one *he* was supposed to come up in.

Suddenly Marcia turned. "Darling," she said, rising quickly.

The hairs on the back of his neck lifted. She wasn't looking straight at him, he felt, but at something behind him. *She was watching him come through the living room.* And she seemed to be quietly enjoying the surprise she knew her nakedness would give him.

Then he realized that she was really looking at him, and that this was Marcia's face to the life, a face vital with awareness, just as he remembered it, and that everything else had been his stupid imagination, and why the devil had he been surprised at her not noticing him sooner when he'd sneaked in so silently?

The surge of relief made his knees shake.

He put out his arms. "Marcia!"

CHAPTER THREE

Shadow of Ecstasy

As CARR WAS about to kiss her, Marcia moved back from him smoothly, hands on his shoulders, inspecting his face.

"You're looking well," she said. "Mix us some drinks while I slip into a dress."

She coolly departed and shut the bedroom door behind him.

Carr located a bottle of rye in the kitchen. Before doing anything else he had a straight shot. The little experience had certainly shaken him up. It was like, but worse than, those moments in childhood when everything seems strangely vivid and at the same time unreal. Chalk on a blackboard. Being outside and through a window watching adults reading newspapers in a living room at night.

He put a tray of ice in the sink to melt, hunted up ginger ale for himself. Marcia of course would take water, not too much.

He'd mention his experience to her, jokingly. On second thought, he wouldn't. At least not right off. Sometimes Marcia wasn't very interested in the subjective. More practical. People, money, the latest news—things like that. Jobs.

He frowned unhappily, remembering her phone call.

He took a long time making the drinks, but the bedroom door was still shut when he brought them out. He sat down, holding them, not touching his. It was a bit like waiting in an office.

When Marcia came in he jumped up, smiling. "Say, are we going to the Pendletons' party Friday? Should be interesting."

She nodded. "You're meeting Keaton Fisher there."

He tried not to hear that.

Marcia sampled her drink. She had put a black slip, but no bra. She sat down on the couch.

"Is it all right?" he asked.

"Of course," she said. "Carr, this idea of Keaton's—"

"Say, Marcia," he began moving over so that he stood in front of her, "the queerest thing happened to me this afternoon."

"—is a remarkable one," she concluded.

He gave up. "Well, what is it exactly?" he asked, starting to sit down close beside her. But she swung around toward him, so that he had to take the other end of the couch, leaving a business-like distance between them.

"In the first place, this is confidential," she began. "Keaton asked me not to tell anyone. You'll have to pretend you're getting it from him first hand, Friday night." She paused. "It's an editorial counseling service."

"What's that?"

"You'll take ailing magazines of all sorts, newspapers, trade journals, etcetera, analyze them and their difficulties, conduct surveys of readers and advertisers, reshape their policies and modernize their methods, pump them full of new ideas—in short, sell them the advice that will put them on their feet."

Carr tried to look thoughtful. Marcia swept on, "Keaton has his plans all laid. He's gone into it very carefully. He's spotted some likely first clients—badly edited publications he knows it'll be easy to improve. That way you'll

29

get a reputation right from the start. Once the circulation of those first publications begins to climb, watch the others flock to you! Even if you have to lose money to turn the trick, it will be worth it."

Carr frowned. "I don't know," he said slowly. "Magazine and newspaper guys have their own ideas. They don't put much trust in the judgment of outsiders."

Marcia smiled with the faintest touch of pity. "Most publishers know that they can't have editorial staffs that are the equal of *Life* or the *Post*, simply because they can't pay the money. But they *can* have an editorial counseling service that's that good, because dozens of other publishers will help to bear the expense."

Carr shrugged. "If we were as good as *Life* or the *Post*, why wouldn't we start a magazine of our own?"

This time Marcia did not smile, although the suggestion of pity was if anything more marked. "Objections, again. Always objections. Next you'll be telling me your interests don't lie in that direction. The time isn't right for new ventures."

"Well," he said, "I can see how all this applies to Keaton Fisher. He's had experience on big magazines. But where do I shine in?"

"It's obvious. Keaton's no good handling people. You're an expert! This service won't be purely an editorial matter. You'll also be reshaping the office routine and personnel of publications."

"I see," he said slowly. "Well, I'll think it over. Say, how about that other drink?"

She pulled back her glass.

"Well, what's wrong with thinking it over? I won't be seeing him until Friday, you say."

"What's wrong?" She sat up straight. "Merely that there's no question of thinking it over at all. You surely don't compare your present job to Keaton's proposition."

He looked at her quickly, then looked away. "Well, Marcia, I don't exactly like the idea of this counseling service."

She smiled, almost encouragingly. "No?"

He sucked his lip. "Oh, it seems too much a part of the old con game. The old business of tailoring wordage, retailoring it, patching it up, cleaning and pressing it, putting it through the mangle over and over again. Too derivative. We wouldn't even be editing the stuff. We'd be editing the editors. Selling them their own product." He

30

hurried on. "No, if I were to break away from General Employment, I'd want it to be for the sake of something more legitimate, more creative."

She leaned back. Carr couldn't recall her ever looking more the cool mistress of herself. Yet he knew she was displaying herself, tempting him deliberately. "Good," she said. "Why don't you?"

"What?"

"Do something creative. You were quite an actor in college, you've told me. Of course it may be a little late for that, though you never can tell. But there's always writing, painting—all sorts of ways of blazoning your personality before the world."

"Oh, Marcia!" For a moment he almost lost control of himself. Then with an effort he put down the hot hunger within him. "Look Marcia, the important thing is that we like each other and have good times together. That's all that really matters, isn't it?" He moved closer to her, watched the rise and fall of her bosom as she breathed.

She did not respond.

"Well, isn't it?" he asked after a moment. "Look, Marcia, I enjoy the times we have together better than anything else. The parties, the shows, the yacht club, all that. Your friends are wonderful. The Pendletons and the Mandevilles are grand people. Last Sunday on the lake was marvelous. There was a kind of glamor in every moment, as there always is when you're around." He slid his hand along the top of the couch, behind her shoulders. "It's fun, don't you see? The best fun in the world?"

"You can't join in the pleasures of people like the Pendletons and the Mandevilles without joining in their enterprises too. In the long run you can't command the sweets of life without commanding people and events."

"Why not?" he asked with simulated lightness. "After all, I pay my own way."

"As an extra man, yes," she admitted without rancor. He was close enough to smell her hair. "But that isn't the same thing at all. Don't you see that you've got to get into the really big money? Why, with all your ability—"

"No, I don't see," he said. "All I can see is you. And I love you very much." Smiling, he quickly put his arms around her and pulled her toward him.

She didn't resist. She only thinned her lips and looked straight into his eyes. "No," she said, "No."

"Please, baby!"

He seized her. With avid roughness he caressed the pink flesh. His kisses fell hot on her throat, her shoulders. He felt the smooth silkiness of her skin, the pliant sweet curves of her filling his palms.

But she jerked back and stood up in one movement. A little of her drink spilled onto the couch and pooled there.

"So that's it," he said. "You tempt me. You entice me. You think if I desire you, you'll control me—I'll do anything you say."

"And if I have to do that to put some steel into your backbone," she replied, "why shouldn't I?"

Carr thought that Marcia had never looked so queenly or desirable. At the same time, he saw in a flash how the whole evening would go from here on. First he would beg her pardon. Then, to please her, he would pretend to become very interested in Keaton Fisher's editorial counseling service. As the evening wore along, what with drinks and the hypnotic glitter of restaurant and nightclub, he actually would begin to get interested. And she would become coolly amorous when he took her home, and let him in, and give him his little reward for dancing to her tune.

Like some puppet. Like some damned puppet dangling on her strings.

Well, for once he wouldn't. For once he'd break the pattern, no matter what it cost him. There were other places he could go tonight. She wasn't his whole life, not quite.

He had backed a couple of steps away from her.

She finished her drink. "I'm ready now," she said, smiling. "I'll get my bag."

As she moved toward the bedroom, he watched her. He swallowed hard. Yes, there were other places. He *had* to prove that.

When she was out of sight, he turned quickly and—the door was still ajar—walked rapidly and silently out of the room and down the hall.

Yes, he kept telling himself, other places.

Short of the elevator, he opened the door to the stairs. He hurried down the gray, squared spiral. Faster. Faster.

Atop his mood of painful desperation, he was aware of a sudden sense of freedom, even excitement. For it had just occurred to him what the other place was. He had just realized the meaning of a phrase he had read uncomprehendingly an hour before: ". . . the lion's tail near the five sisters . . ."

Few people walk on the east side of Michigan Boulevard after dark. At such times the Art Institute looks very dead, with the automobile headlights and he colored glows from the busy side of the boulevard playing on its dark stone like archeologists' flashlights. The two majestic bronze lions might well be guarding the portals of some monument of Roman antiquity. One wonders, though, whether the sculptor Keneys foresaw that the tail of the southernmost lion, conveniently horizontal, would always be kept polished bright by the casual elbows of art students and idlers, and now, the frightened girl.

She watched Carr mount the steps, without any active sign of recognition. He might be part of some dream she was having. A forbiddingly could wind was whipping in from the lake and she had buttoned up her cardigan. She didn't seem so frightened now, but very alone, as if she had nowhere in the world to go and were waiting for someone who would never come. Carr stopped a half dozen paces away.

She smiled and said, "Hello."

Carr walked over to her. His first words surprised him. "I met your small dark man with glasses. He ran away."

"Oh?" she remarked. "I'm sorry. He really is your friend—potentially. But he's rather high strung. Indefinite. He was supposed to meet me here . . ." She glanced toward some distance electric numerals which told the time in order to attract attention to a gigantic bottle of beer.

"Is he afraid of me?" Carr asked.

She shrugged her shoulders. Headlights swept across her gray eyes. At the moment they seemed as enigmatic as those of a sphinx. "I had some vague idea of introducing the two of you," she said. "But now I'm not so sure. About any of us." Her voice dropped. The wind blew some strands of her shoulder-length brown hair against her cheek. "I never really thought you'd come, you know. Leaving notes like that is just a stupid way I have of tempting fate. You weren't supposed to guess. How did you know it was the south lion? I don't think you even looked at the north one."

Carr laughed. "Taft's Great Lakes Fountain is an obsession of mine. I always try to figure out, from the way the bowls the five sisters are holding pour into each other,

33

which sister is which lake. And of course the fountain is nearest the southern lion."

"Did you walk down here tonight?" she asked.

"Yes. And now I have questions for you. Who are those people you warned me against? That big blond, for instance. Why did you let her strike you without doing anything? What sort of hold do they have on you?"

"I don't want to talk about them." Her voice was flat. "It's something obscene and horrible and I don't want to think about it at all."

"Are they after the small dark man with glasses too?"

"I said I don't want to talk about it. It's not something you can do anything about. If you insist on talking about it, I don't want to be with you."

Carr waited. A chillier gust was blowing across the steps and the girl hugged herself.

"All right," he said. "How about us getting a drink somewhere?"

"If you'll let me pick the place."

The last word made him think of Marcia. He quickly linked his arm through the girl's and said, "Lead the way."

At the bottom of the steps he asked, "What's your name?"

"Jane."

"Jane what?"

She shook her head.

"Mine's Carr. Two r's."

They were half a block from the Art Institute when Carr asked, "What about your friend?"

"I don't think there's much chance of his coming now."

They continued north. The wind and the gloom and the wide empty sidewalk seemed strange and lonely so close to the boulevard with its humming cars and its fringe of people and lights on the other side.

Jane's arm tightened a little on Carr's. "This is fun," she said. "I mean—having a date."

"I shouldn't think you'd have any trouble," he told her.

They were opposite the public library. She led them across the boulevard. It seemed to Carr that the loneliness had followed them, for as they walked past the massive dark facade of the library, they met only two people—a galloping, bleak-faced boy and a shffling old man in a checked cap and shabby overcoat.

They squinted against blown grit. A sheet of newspaper flapped into their faces. Carr ripped it away and it swooped up into the air. They looked at each other and laughed. Carr took her hand and started across the next street, under the Elevated.

He felt a sharp tug, heard Jane cry, "Look out!" He jumped back out of the parth of a dark automobile gliding along without lights.

"You should be more careful," she said. "They can't see us, you know."

"Yes," Carr agreed. "The street's awfully dark here."

They walked on a short way. Jane suddenly turned down a cobbled alley chocked with fire escapes. A few steps more and Carr was startled to see the entrance to a little tavern. Steps led down to the sunken door.

The place was dimly lit and almost empty. None of the booths was occupied. At the bar two men were contemplating half-empty glasses of beer. In the shadows were smoky old advertisements and pictures. Carr recognized one—a large print of *Custer's Last Stand*.

"What'll you have?" he asked, heading for the bar.

"Let's wait a minute," she said, steering him instead to the last booth, crowded in like an afterthought beside the swinging door to the kitchen, which was evidently not in use, since the little round window was dark. Neither the two drinkers nor the bartender looked up as they went past. The latter was a solemn and fat man, thoughtfully shaving the foam off a small glass of beer.

Jane looked at Carr across the splotched table. Color had come into her cheeks and she was smiling, as if what they were doing was very wonderful. He found himself thinking of his college days, when there had been hipflasks and roadsters, and checks from home, and classes to cut.

"It's funny," he said, "I've gone past this alley a hundred times and never noticed this place."

"Cities are like that," she said. "You think you know them, when all you know are routes through them. You think that Joe's Hamburgers and the Cleanspot Laundry and Reagan's Mortuary and the woman who's always dusting on the second floor, where the electric wires dip close to the window, are the whole show. One day you turn a corner the wrong way, and after a dozen steps find something you've never seen before."

We're even beginning to talk about life, thought Carr.

One of the beer-drinkers put two nickels in the jukebox. Low, anticipatory strains eddied out.

Carr looked toward the bar. "I wonder if there's a waiter," he said. "Maybe they don't serve at the tables now."

"Who cares?" she said. "Let's dance."

"I don't imagine it's allowed," he said. "They'd have to have another license."

"Come on," she said. He shrugged and followed her.

There wasn't much space, but enough. With what struck Carr as a grave and laudable politeness, the beer-drinkers paid no attention to them, though one softly beat time with the bottom of his glass against his palm.

Jane danced badly, but after a while she got better. Somewhat solemnly they revolved in a modest circle. She was thin. He could feel ribs through the sweater. She said nothing until almost the end of the first number. Then, in a choked voice—

"It's been so long since I've danced with anyone."

"Not with your man with glasses?" he asked quickly.

She shook her head. "He's too nervous, serious all the time. He can't relax—not even pretend."

The second record started. After a while her expression cleared. She rested her cheek against his shoulder. "I've got a theory about life," she said dreamily.

Yes, thought Carr, it's exactly like the old days. He put out of his head the momentary suspicion that she was playing with him—very tenderly, but still playing with him. Like a solemn and wide-eyed child telling a story to an adult.

"I think life has a rhythm," she began, pausing now and then with the music, her phrases drifting. "It keeps changing with the time of day and year, but it's always really the same. People feel it without knowing it, and it governs their lives."

Another couple came in, took one of the front booths. The bartender wiped his hands on his apron, pushed up the wicket in the bar and walked over to them.

"I like your theory, Jane," Carr said. "I like to drift and take things as they come. There's someone who doesn't want me to, who'd like to see me fight the current, build a boat—a heavy cruiser with depth charges. But I'd rather follow the rhythm."

"Oh, but we're not following the rhythm," Jane said. "We've broken away from it."

"Have we?"

"Oh, yes."

36

"Is that what you meant this afternoon when you wondered if I was 'awakened'?"

"Maybe."

The music stopped. Carr dug in his pocket for more nickels to put in the jukebox, but she shook her head. They slid back into their booth.

A telephone rang. The fat bartender carefully put down the tray of drinks he had mixed for the other couple, and went up front to answer it.

"Sure you don't want to dance some more?" Carr asked.

"No, let's just let things happen to us as they come."

"A good idea," Carr agreed, "provided you don't push it too far. For instance, we did come here to get a drink."

"Yes, we did," Jane said. A rather impish expression came into her eyes. She glanced at the two drinks standing on the bar. "Those look good," she said.

Carr nodded. "I wonder what you have to do to get them," he remarked irritably.

"Walk up and take them."

He looked at her. "Seriously?"

"Why not? We were here first. Serve them right." Her eyes were still lively.

He grinned at her. "All right," he said, getting up suddenly, "I will."

She didn't stop him, rather to his surprise. Much more so, there was no squawk when he boldly clutched the two glasses and returned with them to Jane.

She applauded soundlessly.

He bowed and set down the drinks with a flourish. They sipped.

She smiled. "That's another of my theories about life. You can get away with anything if you really want to. Other people can't stop you, because of the rhythm. No matter what happens, they have to keep on dancing. They're stuck. They can only interfere with you if interfering happens to fit the rhythm. Otherwise you're safe."

And rather true, thought Carr. Most people, himself included, went through life in fear and more or less controlled trembling, thinking that if they made the slightest move to assert themselves, they'd be jumped on. They fancied that everyone else was watching them, waiting for them to make a mistake. But actually the other people were as scared as you, or more so. And they rather liked you to make missteps and mistakes, because that eased their worries about themselves. There definitely was a

37

sort of rhythm to life—or at least a counterpoint of opposed timidities. Take that bartender, who was busy with glasses and bottles again. He hadn't even looked in their direction. He was probably embarrassed at having neglected to wait on them, and more relieved than annoyed at what Carr had done.

"Don't you believe me even now?" she pressed. "You *can* get away with things. I'll prove it to you again."

A vague suspicion Carr had entertained when he'd first seen Jane, that she was some sort of shoplifter or petty criminal, flickered again in his mind, only to die immediately.

"You're a funny girl," he said. "What's made you this way? Who's—" He checked himself when she frowned. "Well, here's a question maybe I can ask," he went on. "What startled you so when you sat down at my desk this afternoon? You seemed to sense something in me that terrified you. What was it?"

She shrugged her shoulders. "I don't know." But again her eyes were sphinxlike. "Maybe," she said, "it was just that I realized you were alive."

"That's queer," he said gravely, "because you know, twice today I've had an—an illusion of—"

"Don't," she said, touching his hand. She looked at her glass for a moment, rubbed the beads of moisture, curved her hand around it wonderingly. "It's *good* to be alive," she said intensely. "*Good.* Of course the really marvelous thing would be to be back in the safe old pattern and still alive. But that's impossible."

"And the safe old pattern is. . . ?" he prompted.

She shook her head and looked away. He dropped the question.

More people began to drift in. Carr and Jane finished their drinks, talking about the old advertisements and prints—how they had such a nostalgic feel because, unlike genuine artistic creations, they died with their decade, became dried funeral wreaths and faded love-letters. More people came in. Soon all the other booths were filled and there weren't many empty spaces at the bar. Jane was becoming uneasy.

"Let's go somewhere else," she said abruptly, standing up.

Carr started to say something, but she had slipped around a couple approaching their booth and was striding toward the door. A fear took hold of him that she would get away like this afternoon and he would never see her again. He jerked a dollar bill from his pocketbook and dropped it on the table. With nettling rudeness the newcomers shoved past him and sat down. But there was no time to be sarcastic. Jane was already mounting the stairs. Carr ran after her.

She was waiting outside. He took her arm.

"Do people get on your nerves?" he asked.

She did not answer. It was too dark to see her face. The pavement under their feet was uneven and slippery. He put his arm around her waist.

The alley came to an end. They emerged into a street where the air had that intoxicating glow it displays in the centers of big cities at night. As if the street lamps puffed out clouds of luminous dust which rose three or four stories. Above that, dark walls going up toward a few dull stars.

They passed a music store. Jane's walk slowed to an indecisive drift. Through the open door Carr glimpsed a mahogany expanse crossed by serried walks of ivory and ebony. There were uprights, spinets, baby grands. Jane walked in. The sound of their footsteps died as they stepped onto the thick carpet.

Whoever else was in the store was out of sight somewhere in the back, where a soft glow glamorized shelves of record albums and a row of cubicles. Jane sat down at one of the pianos. Her thin fingers moved for a while over the keys, nervously questing. The taut, talon-suggestive cords in the back of her hands underlined the expression in her face. Then her back stiffened, her head lifted, and there came the frantically rippling, opening arpeggios of the third movement of Beethoven's Moonlight Sonata.

She didn't play it any too well. She struck false notes and the general rendering was somewhat raucous. The impression was that of a student pianist who by a passionate determination has succeeded in grappling passably with a piece beyond her real technical proficiency.

For she did manage to extract from it a feeling of wild, desperate wonder.

Carr stopped speculating as to why a clerk didn't emerge and at least give them a sizing-up glance.

Surely if the composer had ever meant this to be moonlight, it was moonlight illumining a white-pinnacled ocean storm, through rifts in ragged clouds.

Jane's lips were tightly bitten together. Her eyes

seemed to be frantically searching out the next notes in an invisible score. Her body shook as her arms pounded from the shoulders.

Suddenly it was over. In the echoing quiet Carr asked casually, "Is that more like it? The rhythm of life, I mean?"

She made a little grimace as she got up.

"Still too nice," she said. "But there's a hint."

They started out, Carr looking back over his shoulder. "Do you realize we haven't exchanged a word with anyone tonight?" he said.

She smiled wryly. "I think of pretty dull things to do, don't I?" she said, and when he started to protest, "Yes, I'm afraid you would have had a lot more fun with Marcia . . . or with Midge's girl-friend."

"Say, you do have a memory," he said in surprise. "I wouldn't have dreamed you'd—"

He stopped. She had ducked her head. He couldn't make out whether she was crying or laughing.

". . . Midge's girl-friend . . ." he heard her repeat chokingly,

"Don't you know Tom Elvested?" he pressed suddenly.

She disregarded the question and looked up at him with an uneven smile. "But since you *haven't* got a date with anyone but me," she said, "you'll just have to make the best of my antisocial habits. Let's see, this time of night I'm apt to wander off to Rush Street or to South State, to feel the hour and watch the dead faces. I could take you there, or—'"

"That'd be fine," said Carr.

"Or—"

They walked close to the curb, skirting the crowd. They were passing the painfully bright lobby of a movie house, luridly placarded with yellow and purple swirls which seemed to have caught up in their whirlwind folds an unending rout of golden blondes, grim-eyed heroes, money bags, and detached grasping hands. Jane stopped.

"Or I could take you in here," she said.

He obediently veered toward the boxoffice, but she kept hold of his arm and walked him past it into the outer lobby.

"I *will* prove it to you," she told him, half gayly, half desperately, he thought. "I showed you at the bar and the music shop, but—"

Carr shrugged and held his breath for the inevitable.

They walked straight past the ticket-taker and through the center-aisle door.

Carr puffed out the breath and grinned. He thought, maybe she knows someone here.

Or else—who knows?—maybe you *could* get away with almost anything if you did it with enough assurance and picked the right moments.

The theatre was only half full, there were several empty rows at the back. They sidled away into one of these, through the blinking darkness, and sat down. Soon the gyrations of the gray shadows on the screen took on a little sense.

There were a man and woman getting married, or else remarried after a divorce, it was hard to tell which. Then she left him because she thought he was interested only in business. Then she came back, but he left her because he thought she was interested only in social life. Then he came back, but then they both left each other again, simultaneously.

From all around came the soft breathing and somnolent gum chewing of drugged humanity.

Then the man and woman both raced to the bedside of their dying little boy, who had been tucked away in a military academy all this time. But the boy recovered, and then the woman left both of them, for their own good, and a little while afterwards the man did the same thing. Then they boy left them.

"Do you play chess?" Jane asked suddenly.

Carr nodded.

"Come on," she said. "I know a place."

They hurried out of the theatre district into a region of silent gray office buildings.

Carr remarked, "I suppose it must be because they don't have an audience while the picture is being made, that movie actors sometimes seem so unmoved. Havng a real audience puts an actor on the spot."

"Yes," she agreed, her voice fast and low, "watching you every minute, waiting for you to make one false move . . ." Her hand tightened on his arm and she looked up at him. "I hope *you* don't ever have to learn to act that way. I mean when it isn't just a matter of appearing convincing to an audience that, after all, can't really hurt you, but where the slightest slip . . ." She stopped.

"You mean, for instance," said Carr, "as if a person

had been confined, perhaps falsely, in an insane asylum, and then escaped?"

"No," she said shortly, "I don't mean that."

She turned in at a dusky black cave-mouth, flanked by unlighted windows dimly displaying, to the left, knives and other menacing hardware, to the right, behind slim bars, ornate engagement rings. Pushing through a side door next to the locked revolving one, they came into a dingy lobby floored with tiny marble tiles and surrounded by the iron grille-work walls of ancient elevators. A jerkily revolving hand showed that one was still in operation, but Jane headed for the shadow-stifled stair.

"I hope you don't mind," she said. "It's thirteen stories, but I can't stand elevators."

Carr grinned resignedly.

They emerged into a hall where the one frosted door that wasn't dark read: CAISSA CHESS CLUB.

Behind the door was a long room. A drab and careless austerity, untidy rows of small tables, and grimy floor littered with trodden cigarettes, all proclaimed the place to be the headquarters of a somber monamania.

Some oldsters were playing near the door, utterly absorbed in the game. One, with a dirty white beard, was silently kibitzing, occasionally shaking his head, or pointing out, with palsied finger, the move that would have won.

Carr and Jane walked quietly to the far end near the windows, found a box of men as battered by long use as the half-obliterated board, and started to play.

Soon the maddening, years-forgotten excitement had Carr gripped tight. He was back in that relentless little universe where the significance of things is narrowed down to the stratagems whereby turreted rooks establish intangible walls of force, bishops slip craftily past bristling barricades, and knights spring out in sudden sidewise attacks, as if from crooked medieval passageways.

They played three slow, merciless games. She won the first two. Carr was too intent to feel much chagrin. He had never seen a woman play with such sexless concentration. She sat leaning forward in a way that emphasized her slightness—feet on the chair's rung, knees together, head poised like a bird's. One hand held an elbow. From between two fingers of the other, cigarette smoke curled. Her face was at once taut and serene—Carr thought of the portrait bust of Nefertiti, the millenia-dead Egyptian princess—as if Jane had lost herself in a quietness near eternity or the grave.

He finally drew the third game, his king just managing to nip off her last runaway pawn. It felt very late, getting on toward morning, when they finished.

She leaned back, massaging her face.

"Nothing like chess," she mumbled, "to take your mind off things." Then she dropped her hands.

They walked down the stairs. An old woman was wearily scrubbing across the lobby, on her knees, her head bent, as if forever.

In the street they paused uncertainly. It had grown quite cold.

"I'll see you home," said Carr.

Her lips formed the word "No," but she didn't say it. Instead she looked around at him and, after a moment: "All right. But it's a long walk."

The Loop was deserted except for the chilly darkness and the hungry wind. They walked rapidly. They didn't say much. His arm was linked tightly around hers.

They crossed the river over the Michigan Bridge, where the wind had an open channel. Moored, perhaps a block up the river, was a black hulk that looked to Carr like the motor-barge he had seen earlier in the evening. Now it seemed a funeral boat, coffin-shaped, built to carry coffins—a symbol of endings.

Carr's vague notion of making himself a friend of this girl, of solving the mystery of her existence, of helping her to get a real hold on life, died in the cold ebb of night. No. Marcia was his girl—he'd patch things up with her somehow. This was just . . . a weird night.

As if sensing his thoughts, Jane shrank closer to his side.

They turned down a street where big houses hid behind black space and trees. They crossed another street, passing a stylishly archaic lamp with a pane splintered into odd spears. Then the trees closed in again and it grew darker than ever.

She stopped in front of a high iron gate that stood open a couple of feet.

All at once he got the picture his mind had been fumbling for all night. It fitted Jane, her untidy expensive clothes, her arrogant manner. A rich man's daughter, overprotected, neurotic, futilely rebellious, tyrannized by

43

relatives or servants. Everything mixed up, futilely and irremediably, in the way only money can manage.

"It's been so nice," she said in a choked voice, not looking at him. "So nice to pretend. Her small sobs (if they were that) trailed off. Still without looking at him, she squeezed his hand, standing close to him so that that side pressed his, as if gathering courage to leave him and go in. He turned fully toward her, embraced her, and as her face came up, kissed her full on the lips.

She yielded to the kiss and he became aware that he was reacting physically. The need which Marcia had aroused earlier in the evening returned with unexpected force. She made a slight effort to pull away from him. He quickly shifted his hand to the small of her back and pressed her to him, while his other hand dropped hers and carressed the back of her neck while the kiss kept on.

She did pull back then with a gasping chuckle and looked at him, almost comically, a startled question. He nodded ruefully, looked down, and gave a little shrug, as if to say, "I didn't plan on it happening."

"Oh Lord," she said in consternation that was again more comic than not. "Look, Carr, it's much too cold out here and I simply can't ask you in, but I can't leave you like that." A mischievous look came into her eyes and something of her earlier merriment returned as she grabbed his hand. "But first let's get into a little shadow."

And as she tugged him through the gate and toward one of its big pillars, she told him swiftly and eagerly, "When I was twelve years old there was an older boy cousin staying with us and we became great chums. He was going out on his first dates and as you can imagine, I became very interested in his erotic experience, you might say, his amatory progress. When he was on a date I'd stay awake and afterward sneak over to his room to hear how it had gone, whether he'd scored or not, and how. Now wait a minute—"

She had him backed against the side pillar, next to some shrubbery. She searched her small handbag, said, "Damn," under her breath, looked up, he glimpsed something pale slip down into the shubbery, her eyes widened, "Just the thing!" she said with a grin as she impudently snatched his handkerchief from his breast pocket and clipped its corner between his little and ring fingers, then went down with it.

She resumed, "Now when he hadn't scored, which was

44

quite often, and was suffering from it, was all 'het up,' he'd say, he taught me how to fix that up for him, give him a helping hand, as you might say."

Carr chose that moment to begin unbuttoning the top buttons of her cardigan and of the blouse beneath. He felt his zipper being loosened and the cold, cold tips of her first two fingers and her thumb creep to the root of his phallus and walk round it knowingly, sometimes caressing, sometimes probing deeply, sometimes feather-touching. Carr reversed the hand, palm for back, that had done unbuttoning, and thrust it gently down into the warm space between her small, small breasts, then worked out either way to the surprisingly large nipples. Time passed, with more activities. Their cold noses and warm mouths nuzzled each other's face. He feather-touched and felt the aureoles lift and roughen. Her still-cool fingertips moved to his glans and pushed his stretched foreskin all the way back so they could trace the groove around its base. His fingertips darted from nipple to large nipple, patting and pressing each all the way around, while his other hand belatedly slipped down inside her skirt, across her indrawn belly and the surprisingly close-shaven skin below, found her cleft, her clitoris, and caressed it. She drew his foreskin down, then pushed it back. Time raced, more things happened, the pain was exquisite. She gasped, he came and she embraced his coming through his handkerchief. She chuckled and he whinneyed just a little.

Some moment passed and she drew back from him. "Please don't come in with me," she whispered. "And please don't stay and watch."

Carr knew why. She didn't want him to see the lights wink agitatedly on, perhaps hear the beginning of an accusing, rackingly solicitous tirade. It was her last crumb of freedom—to leave him with the illusion that she was free.

He whimsically kissed her helping hand, then took her lightly in his arms. He felt in the darkness the tears on her cold cheek wetting his.

Then she had broken away. There were footsteps running up a gravel drive. He turned and walked swiftly away.

In the sky, through the black trees, shined the first paleness of dawn.

Ecstasy, or the shadow of it, throbbed and undulated in the lightening night.

CHAPTER FOUR

The Big Blonde

THROUGH SLITTED, SLEEP-HEAVY eyes Carr saw the black hands of the clock stiffly invoking the wrath of heaven on all slugabeds. The room was drenched with sunshine.

But he did not hurl himself up. tear into his clothes, rush downtown, just because it was ten minutes past ten.

Nor did he start brooding about how he was going to make his peace with Marcia.

Instead he yawned and closed his eyes, savoring the feeling of independence and self-confidence, the freedom from anxiety, that pervaded him.

Odd that a queer, neurotic girl could give you so much.

Leisurely he pushed his legs out of bed and sat up, rubbing his eyes. Whatever it was she'd given him, he'd certainly needed it. Lord, he'd been getting into a state lately. Not enough sleep, nerves on edge, fighting his job, straining too hard to keep up with the world—until trifles made him tremble, a balmy magnetic inspector reduced him to cowardice, and Marcia's wangling of a magnificent opportunity for him made him run away from her. All that seemed ridiculous now. He had a profound sensation of being back on the right track.

Despite what he owed to it, last night was already becoming hazy in his mind, as if it were an episode that hadn't rightly belonged in his life—a cozy but detached bit of experience framed like a picture.

People ought to have more experiences like that. Helped to break the "rhythm." ·

Grinning, he got up and leisurely bathed and shaved. He'd have breakfast downtown, he decided. Something a little special. Then amble over to the office about the time his regular lunch hour ended.

Sun-warmed, lake-cooled air drifted through the open windows. He rediscovered forgotten pleasures in the stale business of selecting shirt and necktie.

He jogged downstairs. This time the Carr Mackay in the mirror was just a jauntily reassuring counterpart, despite the circled eyes and the gray hairs here and there. He nodded casually.

He'd half thought of permitting himself the luxury of taking a cab to the Loop. But as soon as he got outside he changed his mind. The sun and the air, and the soft brown of the buildings, and the blue of lake and sky, and the general feel of muscle-stretching spring, when even old people crawl out of their holes, were too enticing. He felt fresh. Plenty of time. He'd walk.

The city showed him her best profile. He found pleasure in sensing his own leisurely yet springy bodily movements, in inspecting, as if he were a god briefly sojourning on earth, the shifting scene and the passing people.

If life had a rhythm, Carr thought, it had sunk to a lazy summer murmur from the strings.

His mind idly played over last night's events. He wondered if he could find Jane's home again. An imposing enough place, all right. His guess about her being wealthy had hit the mark.

But he felt no curiosity. Already Jane was beginning to seem like a girl in a dream. They'd met, helped each other, parted. A proper episode. Why did so many people want encounters to lead to something? Often we see people at their best the first time. Why belabor each fresh human contact until it becomes a dull acquaintanceship?

Crossing the Michigan Bridge, he looked around idly for the black motor-barge, but it was nowhere in sight. Far out the lake was dazzling. Next to the bridge, deckhands were washing an excursion steamer. The skyscrapers rose up clean and gray. Cities could be lovely places at times. To crown it, he decided he'd drop into one of the big department stores and make some totally unnecessary purchase. Necktie, perhaps. Say, a new blue.

Inside the store the crowd was thicker. Pausing by the door to spy out the proper counter, Carr had the faintest feeling of oppressiveness.

So low as not to attract general attention, but distinctly audible, came a buzz. Three buzzes, close togehter. Then three more. Carr felt suddenly on the alert, now knowing why.

A large man began to move toward the nearest door, not with obvious haste but not losing any time. Two aisles over another large man was heading in the same direction.

Between them, a well-dressed gray-haired woman was making for the same door with steps a bit faster than seemed appropriate for her bulky figure.

They converged on her. She hurried. They caught up with her at the door.

Superficially, it might have been an aunt being accosted by two polite, solicitous nephews. No one else in the store seemed to realize that anything out of the ordinary was happening.

But Carr noted the hand on the wrist, the gentle prod —it might have been a nephew's love tap—the indignant look and the threat to start a scene on her part, the gentle "It'll be a lot simpler if you don't make a fuss" eyebrow-raising on theirs, the business of escorting her toward the mezzanine stairs—as if the nephews had persuaded their rather flustered aunt to have lunch with them.

Suddenly Carr didn't feel hungry any more. Any thoughts of the subtle pleasures to be derived from idle shopping vanished from his mind. He wanted to get to his place at the office.

It wasn't the incident itself. Nothing extraordinary about that. Just two house detectives picking up a shoplifter when the alarm signal sounded.

It was in what the thing suggested.

It had all happened to inconspicuously. It made you distrustful of crowds and any security you might have thought rested in them.

Outside, the city was noisier, pushier, less friendly.

When Carr got to the office he was annoyed to notice that his heart was pounding and that he was hurrying guiltily. He forced himself to slow down and it turned out that everyone was so busy that no one had time to look up at him or say hello. As he settled down with an exaggerated feeling of relief, his phone buzzed. His heart sank, he didn't know why.

"Morning, Carr."

"Morning." His lips worked. "Marcia, I'm sorry—"

"Head still on?"

"Uh?" Carr's mind fumbled wildly at the remark. It might be sarcasm, but he couldn't figure what sort. Of course he had "lost his head" last night, but—

48

"Well, mine isn't," Marcia continued briskly. "I had a wonderful evening though, in case you're interested."

That cut. Marcia lost no time in punishing people, all right. Still he had it coming to him. "Marcia, I acted like a fool," he began.

"Simply wonderful. Never known the food to be better at the Kungsholm."

She said it in the pleasantest sort of voice. No suggestion that she was trying to hurt him.

"And afterwards—that was marvelous too."

Carr winced. The easy confidence he'd felt toward Marcia earlier in the morning evaporated. He felt altogether jealous and miserable.

"Listen, Marcia, I told you I acted like a fool—"

"What I wanted to call you about," she interrupted, "was that I'm glad you've decided to change your mind about Keaton Fisher."

The phone was silent. Carr got the point, or thought he did. She'd forgive him, if he'd go after the Fisher job. Well, that was all right, he'd come around to that way of thinking himself. But he hated to let her believe she'd forced him into it. Still—

"I *have* changed my mind, Marcia," he said.

"And I want you to make a really good impression on him Friday night."

"I'll try."

"I know you will. Goodbye, darling."

He replaced the receiver. Well, that was that. He'd committed himself. Probably for his own good.

Might have known Marcia would get her way in the end. He wondered what man she'd gone out with last night, decided he ought to put that question out of his mind.

"Coming?"

He looked up. People had their hats on and were going to lunch. Tom Elvested was standing beside his desk.

"Sure, sure," Carr said hurriedly. "Be right with you."

Going over to the Italian's, his mood brightened. After all, he'd made his peace with Marcia, even though at a price. Something of the calm elation he'd felt earlier in the morning returned to him. He was half of a mind to tell Tom about last night, yet felt a queer reticence. Plenty of reason for feeling that way, though, he told himself. For one thing, he didn't want it to get back to Marcia. For another, if he described it to Tom, it would seem just

49

silly. Finally, there was his persistent impression that Jane knew Tom, was connected with him in some way, and right now he didn't want to know any more about her or get involved with her in any way.

So when they'd found a table at the Italian's and decided that the veal cutlet *parmigiana* looked the best, and Tom asked, "How was your date with Marcia?" Carr merely said, "Swell." He hurried on to ask in turn, "And how did you get along with Midge and her girlfriend?"

"Her friend didn't come. We couldn't scare up another date for her at short notice. Midge tried to persuade her to come anyway, but I guess she was afraid of spoiling our twosome."

"I'm sorry," said Carr. "If it hadn't been for my date with Marcia . . . and of course, you did ask me at the last minute."

"Sure," said Tom, tearing off bits of French bread and dropping them in his cup of minestroni. "Still, I'd like you to meet her some day. I think you and she have a lot in common."

"What way?" Carr asked.

Tom fished up a spoonful of sopping bits of bread. "Oh, your more submerged qualities," he said.

Carr looked at him for a moment, decided not to follow that one up. Might as well begin working up enthusiasm about his new future, it occurred to him. "Say, you know, Marcia's got on to something very interesting," he began, and while they were finishing their soup, he outlined Keaton Fisher's plan for an editorial counseling service. The cutlets came and they were both busy for a while. Then, when Tom was wiping up the last of the tomato sauce with a fragment of bread on his fork, Carr asked, "Well, what do you think of it?"

Tom chewed his bread before replying. Then he countered uninspiredly, "Are you sure it's the sort of job you'd like?"

"Oh, hell," Carr said, "you know that we probably wouldn't be employment men if we were certain of the job we wanted."

Tom grinned. "I grant you that. Just as the psychiatrist is apt to be a little crazy. But I've got an angle about you. I don't think you like people."

"Really?"

"No. Now me, I may be no great shakes at personnel work, but still I like people. I like to speculate about them. I even like to relax with them. I'm uneasy if they're not around. But you—I think people get on your nerves. You conceal it pretty well, but I've caught you looking at people as if they irritated the hell out of you. It's almost as if you felt they were queer little machines that were bothering you."

"Oh, hell," Carr said.

"Maybe, but all the same there's something eating you."

"And all of us."

Tom sipped his coffee. "Well, in that case Keaton's idea certainly sounds like it might be a gold mine," he admitted, as if honestly impressed.

But there was a certain uncomfortableness between them and it lingered as they returned to the office. Damn it, Carr thought, Tom's all wet about my not liking people. What I don't like is the conditions under which we meet most people today—the superficiality of the contact, the triteness of ideas exchanged, and the synthetic, movie-and-radio shaped nature of the feelings involved.

He was tempted to tell Tom about Jane, to show him he could enter into the spirit of people. But he was afraid Tom might turn the argument against him by pointing out that he and Jane had behaved like two typically lonely, unsociable people.

No, he wouldn't ever discuss Jane with anyone. It was one of those things. Over and done with. Something that would have no consequences whatever.

He and Tom climbed the one flight to General Employment. Carr stopped at the men's room. A minute later, entering the applicants' waiting room, he looked through the glass panel and saw the big blonde who had slapped Jane sitting in his swivel chair, rummaging through the drawers of his desk.

CHAPTER FIVE

Trail of Desire

CARR DIDN'T MOVE. His first impulse was to confront the woman, but right on its heels came the realization that she'd hardly be acting this way without some sort of authorization—and hardly obtain an authorization without good cause.

His mind jumped back to his fleeting suspicion that Jane was mixed up in some sort of crime. This woman might be a detective.

On the other hand, she might have walked into the office without anyone's permission, trusting to bluff—her very brassiness and self-assurance—to get away with it.

Carr studied her from behind the glass panel. She was undeniably beautiful. With that lush figure, faultless blonde hair, and challenging lips, she might be a model for billboard advertisements. Even the slight out-of-focus look of her eyes didn't spoil her attractiveness. And her gray sports outfit looked like a high-class hundred dollars or so.

Yet there was something off-key, unpleasantly exaggerated, overripe about even her good looks and get-up. She carried the lush figure with a blank animal assurance; there was unhidden cruelty in the challenging lips, there was an unashamed barbarousness in the two big silver pins piercing her mannish gray sports hat. She seemed utterly unconcerned with and contemptuous of the people around her. She glanced through Carr's folders with the cold detachment of a biologist examining cancer slides. If ever there was a woman who gave the impression of simply using people, of using the world, this was she. Carr felt strangely cowed.

But the situation was getting impossible, he told himself. Tom, apparently busy with some papers at the next desk, must be wondering what had happened to him and what the devil the woman was up to.

Just then the blonde dropped back a folder, shut a drawer, and stood up. Carr faded back into the men's room. He waited perhaps fifteen seconds, then cautiously stepped out. The woman was no longer in sight. He looked into the outside corridor. It was empty. He hadn't heard the elevator for the last few seconds. He ran to the head of the stairs. He spotted the gray sports coat going through the revolving door. He hurried down the stairs, hesitated a moment, then darted through the lobby entrance into the small tobacco and magazine store adjoining. He could probably still catch a glimpse of her through the store's show window. In any case, it would be less conspicuous than dashing right out on the sidewalk.

The store was empty except for a middle-aged man who, in the proprietor's absence, was coolly leaning across the counter and helping himself to a package of cigarettes. Carr ignored this slightly startling scene and moved quietly toward the window. With commendable nerve—or perhaps he was a bit deaf—the middle-aged man tore open the filched pack without looking around. He was well-dressed and inclined to portliness.

Just then Carr glimpsed a patch of familiar gray approaching and realized that the blonde woman was coming into the tobacco shop from the street.

The lobby door was too far away. Carr sidled behind a magazine rack.

The first voice he heard was the woman's. It was as disagreeably as her manner.

"I searched his desk. There wasn't anything suspicious."

"And of course you did a good job?" The portly man's voice was quite jolly. "Took your time? Didn't miss anything?"

"Of course."

"Hm." Carr heard a match struck and the faint crackle of a cigarette igniting. iHs face was inches away from a line of luridly covered magazines.

"What are you so worried about?" The woman sounded quarrelsome. "Can't you take my word for it? Remember, I checked on them yesterday."

"Worry pays, Miss Hackman, as you'll discover when you've been in the situation a bit longer." The portly man sounded pleasanter than ever. "We have strong reason to suspect the girl. I respect your intelligence, but

53

I'm not completely satisfied. We'll do another check on the girl tonight."

"Another? Aren't we supposed to have any time for fun?"

"Fun must be insured, Miss Hackman. Hardly be fun at all, would it, if you felt someone might spoil it? And then if some other crowd should catch on . . . No, we'll do another check."

"Oh, all right." The woman's voice expressed disgusted resignation. "Though I suppose it'll mean prowling around for hours with the beast."

"Hm. No, I hardly think the beast will be necessary, Miss Hackman."

Carr, staring sightlessly at the pulp and astrology magazines, felt his flesh crawl. It wasn't so much the murky import as the utter matter-of-factness of the conversation.

"Why not let Dris do it?" he heard the woman say. "He's had the easy end lately."

"Hm. That's a possibility, all right. We'll think it over." The portly man's voice was moving toward the street door. "Best be getting on now."

Several seconds later Carr peered around the rack. Through the window he could see the big blonde and the portly man entering a black convertible. The driver was a bored-looking young man with a crew haircut. As he turned toward the others, throwing his right arm along the top of the seat, Carr saw that it did not end in a hand, but a hooked contrivance. He felt a thrill of recognition. These were the three people Jane had mentioned in her note, all right. ". . . affable-seeming older man . . ." Yes, it all fitted.

The driver had his hand hook on the wheel, but the car didn't move yet. All there of them seemed to be discussing something. Again Carr got that intimidating impression of power he'd had when watching the woman upstairs.

The driver seemed to lose interest in the discussion. Turning sideways again, he dangled his hook into the back seat. There was a flash of glistening black, which instantly vanished. Carr felt another shiver crawling along his back. Perhaps the driver had merely flirted up the corner of a black fur driving robe. But this was almost summer and the black flash had been very quick.

The middle-aged man seemed to speak sharply to the

54

driver. The convertible began to move. Carr hurried to the window. He got there in time to see the convertible swinging around the next corner, rather too swiftly for sensible downtown driving.

He stood there for a few seconds, then turned around. The proprietor had returned, but Carr ignored him. He slowly walked upstairs.

He hesitated at Tom's desk. He had half an impulse to tell Tom about things, ask him about the woman, but the big Swede was busy with an applicant. Another applicant was approaching his own desk. Frowning, he sat down.

He felt extremely puzzled, disturbed. Above all, he wanted to think things through, but as luck would have it the afternoon turned out to be a busy one.

Yet through all the details of job histories and qualifiations, references and referral slips, his thoughts—or rather his sensations—kept wandering. At one time it would be a remembered phrase: "Worry pays," "Fun must be insured," "I hardly think the beast will be necessary." At another it was the pulp magaines on the rack downstairs; he hadn't remembered seeing them at the time, but now their covers stood out very clearly in his mind. He could read the frantic titles. Once he had the momentary feeling that the portly man had walked into his office. And for several minutes he was bothered by something black and rough poking now and then around the end of one of the benches in the waiting room, until he looked more closely and saw it was a woman's handbag.

With a slump of relief he watched the last applicant depart. He'd thought she was going to keep on talking forever—and it was a minute past quitting time and the other interviewers were hurrying for their hats and wraps.

His glance lit on a scrap of pencil by the wire basket on his desk. He rolled it toward him with one finger. It was fiercely chewed, making him think of nails bitten to the quick. He recognized it as the one Jane had dropped on his desk yesterday.

Damn it all, he didn't want to get mixed up in anything. Not now that he'd made his peace with Marcia and ought to be concentrating on the Keaton Fisher proposal. He'd let jumpy nerves get the better of him yesterday, he didn't want what to happen again. The rather ridiculous episode with Jane was something that ought to remain a closed incident. And how was he going to warn her even if he wanted to? He didn't even know her last name.

Besides, it didn't sound as if those three people actually wanted to harm her, when you came to analyze the conversation he'd overheard downstairs. They'd spoken of "checking" on her. The impression was that they were afraid she might harm them, rather than the reverse. References to a "beast," though admittedly grisly-sounding at the time, were probably some figure of speech. The "beast" might be merely a disliked person, or an automobile, or even a camera or suitcase.

Furthermore, Jane had intimated several times that she didn't want him to learn about or interfere with the three people against whom she'd warned him, that it might mean danger to her if he did. What was it she'd said about them? "horrible and obscene. . . . ?"

Who could they be and what could they be up to? Secret agents of some sort? Loads of people were being "checked" today. Yet there's been that mention of "some other crowd," that talk about "fun." Still, presumably even secret agents wanted to have "fun" occasionally.

Jane was wealthy, he'd guessed. But again these people didn't sound as if they were out for money, only some sort of security, so they could have their "fun" in perfect safety.

"Fun" in perfect safety . . . Once again there came back that tremendous impression of ruthless power the three had given him. His desk invaded, his file folders searched . . . The stolen cigarettes . . . The slap . . . No, damn it, he couldn't drop it here. Whatever Jane had intimated, it was his duty to tell her what he'd overheard, to warn her about tonight.

And there was a perfectly obvious way of doing it. He knew where she lived, since last night. He'd go out there right now.

He stood up, only now noticing that the office had emptied itself while he'd been thinking. The cleaning woman, dry mop over her shoulder, was pushing in a cart for the wastepaper. She ignored him.

Carr grabbed his hat and walked out past her, tramped down the stairs.

Outside the day had stayed sparklingly fair, so that, instead of yestday's gloom, the street were flooded with a soft white light that imparted a subdued carnival atmosphere to the eager hurry of the rush hour. Distant faces stood out with unnatural distinctness, as if seen through the wrong end of a telescope. Voices hung on the air. The general clatter sounded almost jolly. Streets and shop windows were colorful with mannequins ogling the paychecks of Spring.

Carr felt a touch of dancing, adventurous excitement begin to add itself to his tension. Instead of heading over to Michigan Boulevard, he took a more direct route northward, crossing the sluggish river by one of the blacker, more nakedly girde red bridges. The sky here spread out big, above vast remote walls formed by windowless warehouses and office buildings with ornate marble, gilt, or ebony spires. Westward loomed the railway yards, a black expanse studded with grim, baffling structures that looked capable of lifting locomotives and maybe did just that.

Beyond the river, the street slanted downward into a region where the economic tides of the city moved at their shallowest and rapidest. The small, ill-washed shopwindows were mostly those of beaneries with unappetizing tiers of hot dogs, second-hand magazine stores, small saloons that were all blacked-out window and beer advertisements, check-cashing cubby-holes, drug stores with screaming displays laid out six months ago. Overhead, crammed apartments. Here and there, a soot-darkened church with shut doors.

This kept up for some eight or ten blocks without much change except an increasing number of cramped nightclubs with winking blue signs and tiredly smiling photographs of the girls who presumably disbursed the "continuous entertainment."

Then, in one block, by the stern sorcery of zoning laws, the squalid neighborhood was transformed into a wealthy residential section. First a few apartment hotels, massive, aloof, with the first story dark and barred like old city strongholds of Florence or Venice. Then heavy-set houses with thickly curtained windows, their fenced and untrod lawns suggesting the cleared areas around forts, the shrubs like *cheval-de-frise*.

If memory served him right, Jane's house lay just a block and a left turn ahead.

But now, for the first time, Carr's footsteps lagged. It occurred to him that he might have to give his warning under rather difficult circumstances. What if her parents wouldn't let him see Jane, or at least demanded a preliminary explanation? He'd have to tell about last night and would Jane want that? Just a fellow she'd picked up, who didn't even know her last name (unless he found it on the mailbox).

He quickened his step. Such speculations were futile, he told himself. He'd have to gauge the situation when he got there, invent suitable lies if necessary.

He rounded the corner, nothing a broken street lamp. He remembered the odd pattern of its cracks from last night.

He came to a high fence of iron and brick, to a tall gate of twisted grillework which he recognized.

He stopped dead, stared, took a backward step.

This couldn't be it. He must have made a mistake.

But the spears of broken glass in the street lamp could not have been duplicated, nor, hardly, this elaborate gate.

The sunken sun, reaching a point from which its rays were reflected from the underside of a cloudbank, suddenly sent a spectral yellow afterglow. Everything was very clearly illuminated. Nothing was lost in shadow.

A gravel drive led up to just the sort of big stone mansion he had imagined—turreted, slate-roofed, heavy-eaved, in the style of 1890's.

But the gate and fence were rusty, tall weeds encroached on the drive, lawn and flowerbeds were a wilderness, the upper windows were blank and curtainless, most of them broken, those on the first floor were boarded up and the door as well. Pigeon droppings whitened the somber brown stone, and in the center of the lawn, half hidden by the weeds, stood a weather-bleached sign:

FOR SALE

58

CHAPTER SIX

Gigolo's Home

CARR PUSHED DOUBTFULLY at the iron gate. It opened a couple of feet, then squidged to a stop against gravel still slightly damp from yesterday's rain. He stepped inside.

The house seemed unquestionably deserted. Still, recluses have been known to live in unlikely places.

Or a place like this might be secretly used by intruders. Eyes might even now be peering through the cracks between the boards covering the lower windows.

His feet were carrying him up the driveway, which led back behind the house, passing under a porte-cochere. He had almost reached it when he noticed the footprints.

They were a woman's, quite fresh, and yet sunk more deeply than his own. They must have been made since the rain. There were two sets, one leading toward the porte-cochere, the other back from it.

Looking at the black ruined flowerbeds, inhaling their dank odor, Carr was relieved that there were footprints.

He examined them more closely. Those leading toward the porte-cochere were deeper and more widely spaced. He remembered that Jane had been almost running.

But the most startling discovery was that the footprints never reached the house at all. They stopped in the mud of blown dirt under the porte-cochere a good six feet from the soil-streaked steps. They cluttered confusedly there, then they returned toward the gate. Evidently Jane had run under the porte-cochere, waited until she was sure he was gone, then retraced her steps.

She apparently had wanted him to think that she lived in a mansion.

He walked back to the gate. A submerged memory from last night was tugging at his mind. He looked along the iron fence fronting the sidewalk. A scrap of paper just inside caught his eyes. It was lodged in the low black shoots of some leafless shrub.

He remembered something white fluttering from Jane's handbag in the dark, drifting down.

He worked his way to it, pushing between the fence and the shrubbery. Unpruned shoots caught at his coat.

The paper was twice creased and the edges were yellowed and frayed, as if it had been carried around for a long time. It was not rain-marked. Unfolding it, he found the inside filled with a brown-inked script vividly recalling Jane's scribbled warning, yet much smaller and more crabbed, as if a pen were to her a chisel for carving hieroglyphs. With some difficulty, holding the paper up and moving toward the center of the tangled lawn to catch the failing light, he read:

Always keep up appearances.
Always be doing something.
Always be first or last.
Always be on the streets or alone.
Always have a route of escape.
Avoid: empty stores, crowded theaters, restaurants, queues.
Safe places: libraries, museums, churches, bars.
Never hesitate, or you're lost.
Never do anything odd—it wouldn't be noticed.
Never move things—it makes gaps.
Never touch anyone—DANGER! MACHINERY!
Never run—they're faster.
Never look at a stranger—it might be one of them.
These are the signs: contemptuousness, watchfulness, bluff; unveiled power, cruelty, lust; they use people; they are incubi, succubi. No one ever really notices them—so don't you.
Some animals are really alive.

Carr looked over his shoulder at the boarded-up house. A bird skimmed up from the roof. It looked leaner than a pigeon. Perhaps a nighthawk. Somewhere down the block footsteps were clicking on concrete.

He considered the shape of the paper. It was about that of an envelope and the edges were torn. At first glance the other side seemed blank. Then he saw a faded postmark and address. He struck a match and, shielding it with the paper, made out the name—Jane Gregg; and the city—Chicago. The postmark was a little more than a year old. The address, lying in a crease, presented more difficult, but he deciphered it: 1924 Mayberry Street.

The footsteps had come closer. He looked up. Beyond the fence a couple was passing. He could see a bit of white wing-collar and the glitter of a sequined comb. The gait was elderly. He guiltily whipped out the match, but they walked by without turning their heads.

After a moment he slipped through the gate, pulled it shut, and set out in the same direction they were going, cutting across the street before he passed them.

The street lights winked on. The leaves near the lights looked an artificial green. He walked faster.

In this direction there was no abrupt zone-wall, but rather a gradual deterioration. The houses shouldered closer to each other, grew smaller, crept toward the street. The trees straggled, gave out, the grass died. Down the cross-streets neon signs began to glow, and the drone of busses, radios and voices grew in volume. Suddenly the houses coalesced, reached the sidewalk with a rush, shot up in towering brick combers, became the barracks of the middle classes, with only a narrow channel of sidewalk between their walls and the rows of cars parked bumper to bumper.

Carr thought wryly of his shattered theory of thick-carpeted halls, candlelight and a persecuted heiress. Mayberry Street wasn't that.

The strange notes Jane had inked on the envelope kept flashing in his consciousness. If anything had ever read more like a paranoid's rulebook—! And yet . . .

A bent yellow street-sign said *Maxwell*. At the next corner, *Marston*. Then, following the mindless association pattern that so often governs the selection of street names, *Mayberry*.

He looked at the gold numerals painted on the glass door of the first apartment house. They were 1954-58.

As he went down the street, he had the feeling that he was walking back across the years.

The first floor of 1922-24 was lighted on the 24 side, except for a small dark sun-porch. Behind one window he noticed the edge of a red-upholstered davenport and a gray-haired man in shirtsleeves reading a newspaper. Inside the low-ceilinged vestibule he turned to the brass letter boxes on the 24 side. The first one read: *Herbert*

Gregg. After a moment he pushed the button, waited, pushed it again.

There was no response, neither a mumble from the speaking tube, nor a buzz from the lock of the door to the stairs.

Yet the "Herbert Gregg" apartment ought to be the one in which he had seen the old man sitting.

Beyond the inner door, in the darkness of the stair well, he thought he saw something move. He couldn't tell what it was. When he stepped closer and peered in, he saw nothing.

He went outside. He craned his neck. The man was still sitting there. An old man—perhaps deaf?

Then, as Carr watched, the man put down his paper, settled back, looked across the room, and from the window came the opening triplets of the first movement of the Moonlight Sonata.

Carr felt the wire that fenced the tiny, nearly grassless plot press his calf and realized that he had taken a backward step. He reminded himself that he'd only heard Jane play the third movement. He couldn't know she'd play the first just this way.

He went back into the vestibule, again pushed the button.

There was no faltering of the piano notes. They sounded icy, remote, inhuman, as if some huge insect were treading neatly, courtseyingly, infallibly up and down the keyboard.

Carr again peered through the inner door. Light trickled down from the second landing above. He tried the door. Someone must have left it off the buzzer, for it opened.

He hurried past the blackness of the bottom of the stair well. Five steps, a turn, five steps more. Then, just as he reached the first landing, which still wasn't very light, he felt something small and silent come brushing up against his ankle from behind.

His back and hands pressed to the plaster wall.

Then he relaxed. Just a cat. A black cat with a white throat and chest, like evening clothes.

And a very cool cat too. It walked suavely toward the door of the Gregg apartment.

But about two feet away it stopped. For several seconds it stood there, head upraised, making no movement, except its fur seemed to thicken a little. Then, very slowly, it looked around.

It stared at Carr.

Beyond the door, the piano started the sprightly second movement.

Carr edged out his hand. His throat felt dry and constricted. "Kitty," he croaked.

The cat arched its back, spat, then made a twisting leap that carried it halfway up the next semi-flight of stairs. It crouched on the top step, its bugged green eyes peering between the rails of the bannister.

There were footsteps. Without thinking, Carr shrank back. The door opened, the music suddenly swelled, and a gray-haired lady in a blue and white print dress looked out and called, "Gigolo! Here, Gigolo!"

She had Jane's small chin and short straight nose, behind veils of plumpness. Not Jane's height, though. She was rather dumpy. Her face had a foolish look.

And she must be short-sighted, for although she looked at the stairs, she didn't see the cat, nor did she notice Carr. Feeling uncomfortably like a prowler, he started to step forward, then realized that she was so close he would give her a fright.

"Gigolo!" She called again. Then, to herself, "That cat!" A glance toward the dead bulb in the ceiling and a distracted headshake. "Gigolo!"

She backed inside. "I'm leaving it open, Gigolo," she called. "Come in when you want to."

Carr stepped out of the darkness with a husky, "Excuse me," but the opening notes of the fast third movement, played too loudly, drowned him out.

He crossed to the door. The green eyes at the top of the stairs followed him. He raised his hand to knock. But at the same time he looked through the half-open door, across a tiny hall, into the living room.

It was a smallish room, with too much heavy furniture in addition to the fake fireplace, and too many lace runners on little tables and antimacassars on the head rests and arms of chairs. He could see the other end of the red davenport and the slippered feet of the old man sitting in it. The woman had retired to a straight-backed chair across the room and was sitting with her hands folded, her lips worriedly pursed.

Between them was the piano, an upright. On top of it was a silver-framed picture of Jane.

But there was no one sitting at the piano.

To Carr, the rest of the room seemed to darken and curdle as he started at the rippling keys.

Then he puffed out his breath. Of course, it was some kind of electric player.

He started to knock, then hesitated because they were listening to the music.

The woman moved uneasily on her chair. Her lips kept anxiously puckering and relaxng, like those of a fish behind aquarium glass.

Finally she said, "Aren't you tiring yourself, dear? You've been at it all day, you know."

Carr looked toward the man, but he could still see only the slippered feet. There was no reply.

The piano stopped. Carr took a step forward. But just then the woman got up and went over to the piano. He expected her to do something to the mechanism, but instead she began to stroke the air a couple of feet above the piano bench with a downward patting motion.

Carr felt himself shivering.

"There, there, dear," she said, her face showing that silly, vacant expression he had oticed at the door, "that was very pretty, I know, but you're really spending too much time on your music. At your age a girl ought to be having fun, meeting other young people. But you keep yourself cooped up." She leaned forward, bent her head as if she were looking around the shoulder of someone seated at the piano, wagged her finger, and said with a sickly playfulness, "Look at the circles under those eyes."

The slippered feet protruding from the red davenport twisted. A weary voice said, "Now don't worry yourself over Jane, Mother."

The woman straightened. "Too much practicing is bad for anyone. It's undermining her health—and I don't care how ambitious she is, or how ambitious you are for her."

The slippered feet were drawn back. The davenport creaked. The man came into sight, not quite as old as Carr had thought, but tired-looking. His shirt, open at the neck, was made for a detachable collar.

For Carr, time stopped, as if a clockworks universe hesitated before the next tick. In that frozen pause, only his thoughts moved. It was true, then. The dumpy man . . . The room clerk . . . Marcia in her bedroom . . . Last night with Jane—the bar, the music shop, the movie house, the chessplayers . . . And now this old woman.

All, all automata, machines!

Or else (time moved again) this old woman was crazy.

Yes, that was it. Crazy, insane. Behaving in her insanity as if her absent daughter were actually there. Believing it.

He clung to that thought.

"Really dear," the old woman was saying vapidly, "you simply must rest."

"Now, mother, don't get excited," the old man said soothingly. "Everything's all right."

The father insane too, Carr thought. No, humoring her. Pretending to believe her hallucinations. That must be it.

"Everything isn't all right," she contradicted tearfully. "I won't have Jane practicing so much and taking those wild long walks by herself. Jane, you mustn't—" Suddenly a look of fear came over her. "Oh, Jane, don't go. Please don't go, Jane." She stretched out her hand toward the hall as if to restrain someone. Carr shrank back. He felt sick. It was horrible that this mad old woman should resemble Jane.

She dropped her hand. "She's gone," she said and began to sob.

The man put his arm around her shoulder. "You've scared her off," he said softly. "But don't cry, mother, please don't cry. Tell you what, mother, let's go sit in the dark for a while. It'll rest you." He urged her toward the sun porch.

Just then, behind Carr, the cat hissed and retreated a few steps higher, the vestibule door downstairs was banged open, there were loud footsteps, and voices raised in argument.

"But I tell you, Mr. Wilson, you're just wasting our time. Dris checked. He told us so."

"He lied. He'd been with those girls two hours when we saw him."

"He hadn't!"

"You think not?"

The first voice was brassy, complaining. The second was cool, jolly. They were those Carr had overheard in the cigarette shop.

Before he had time to weigh his fear or even to think

coherently at all, he had slipped through the door in front of him, crossed the little hall as rapidly as he dared—Jane's parents were out of the living room by now—tiptoed down the hallway leading to the back of the apartment, turned into the first room he came to, and was standing with his cheek to the wall, squinting back the way he had come.

He couldn't quite see the front door. But in a little while long shadows darkened the plaster of the hallway, telling him that someone must be standing in the hall, cutting off the light from the living room.

"Well, she isn't here," he heard Mr. Wilson say.

"But we just heard her playing," came the blonde's voice, naggingly.

"Be reasonable, Miss Hackman," Mr. Wilson objected. "You know very well that doesn't prove anything."

"But why would Dris lie about checking on her?"

Mr. Wilson snorted. 'Dris would lie about anything to get time to be with his current girls."

"That's not true!" Miss Hackman sounded as if the remark had stung. "Dris might fool around with girls when we're all having fun together. Naturally. But not just by himself, not alone!"

"You think he doesn't have his private lusts? You think you're the whole show?"

"Yes!"

"Ha!"

Carr waited for the footsteps or voices of Jane's parents. Surely they must be aware of the intruders. The sun porch wasn't that isolated.

Perhaps they were as terrified as he.

Or perhaps—no, damn it, that idea he'd had (when time had stopped) couldn't, mustn't be true.

"You're not being fair," Miss Hackman whined. "The girl's probably somewhere in the back of the house. Let's look."

Carr had already stooped and unwhipped the knots of his shoelaces. Now he stepped out of his shoes. The room he was in contained twin beds. Light poured into it from a white-tiled bathroom. There was the same fussiness and profusion of bric-a-brac in the bedroom as in the living room.

One of the shadows in the hall drew darker. But just as Carr was starting for the bathroom, he heard Mr. Wilson snap a command.

"Stop! The sun porch! Listen to the old woman! What's she saying?"

In the ensuing silence Carr could hear a faint mumbling.

"You see," Mr. Wilson whispered loudly. "She's talking as if the girl were there."

"But—"

"Listen!"

The mumbling stopped.

"Do you need any more proof?" Mr. Wilson demanded. After a moment he went on, his voice smooth again. "I know about your tender feelings for Dris, Miss Hackman. As feelings, they mean nothing to me. As influences warping your judgment, they mean a great deal. Dris is very clever at times, but slack. You know that our pleasures, our plans, our very existence, depend on constant vigilance. We could be wrecked by one single person, such as this girl, or the little man with glasses."

"He's dead," Miss Hackman interposed.

"That's wishful thinking. Suppose he or the girl become actively hostile. Worse, suppose they inform another and stronger group like ourselves—there are such, believe me!—of our existence. You and I *know*, Miss Hackman, that girl knows about us—"

"I think she's gone back into her old rut," Miss Hackman interrupted, "and we don't have to worry about her. That can happen. Most of them want to go back."

Trying to catch a glimpse of the talkers, Carr began to edge closer to the door, noiseless in his stocking feet.

"But the mother . . . ?" Mr. Wilson was saying.

"Crazy. So she thinks the girl's there."

Mr. Wilson's shadow nodded. "I'll grant you that—as a possibility. The girl perhaps has gone back into her rut. But perhaps she hasn't. Perhaps she's taken up with Dris, or he with her, on the sly."

"Oh no! That's indecent! If I repeat to Dris what you just said—"

"Still, wouldn't you like proof that it isn't so?"

"I wouldn't lower myself to entertain such a contemptible suspicion!"

"You wouldn't, eh? You don't sound—*What's that!*"

Carr stiffened. Looking down, he saw that he had knocked over a stupid little doorstop in the form of a porcelain pekinese sitting up to beg. He started for the bathroom door, but he had hardly taken the first painfully cautious step when he heard, from that direction, faintly, but unmistakably, the sound of someone else moving around. He froze, then turned toward the hall. He heard the stamp of high heels, a little throaty exclamation of surprise from Mr. Wilson, a softly pattering rush, the paralyzing fighting squall of a cat, a flailing of shadows, a smash and clatter as if a cane or umbrella had been brought down on a table, and Mr. Wilson's exclamation:

"Damn!"

Next Carr caught a glimpse of Miss Hackman. She had on a pearl grey evening dress, off the shoulders, and a mink wrap over her arm. She was coming down the hall, but she didn't see him.

At the same moment something launched itself at her from behind. The cat Gigolo landed in the faultless golden hair, claws raking. Miss Hackman screamed.

The ensuing battle was too quick and confused for Carr to follow it clearly, and most of it took place in the little hall, out of sight except for the shadows. Twice more the cane or umbrella smashed down, Mr. Wilson and Miss Hackman shouted and yelled at each other at the same time, the cat squalled continually. Then Mr. Wilson shouted, "The door!" there came a final whangling blow, followed by Mr. Wilson's "Damn!"

For the next few moments, only heavy breathing from the hallway, then Miss Hackman's voice, rising to a vindictive wail: "Bitch! Look what it did to my cheek. Oh, why must there be cats!"

Then Mr. Wilson, grimly businesslike: "It hasn't got away. It's trapped on the stairs. We can get it."

Miss Hackman: "This wouldn't have happened if we'd brought the beast!"

Mrs. Wilson: "The beast! This afternoon you thought differently. Do you remember what happened to Dris?"

Miss Hackman: "That was his own fault. He shouldn't have teased it. Besides, the beast likes me."

Mr. Wilson: "Yes, I've seen her look at you and lick her chops. We're wasting time, Miss Hackman. You'll have a lot more than a scratched cheek—or a snapped-off hand—to snivel about if we don't clear up this mess right away. Come on. We've got to kill that cat."

Carr heard footsteps, then the sound of Mr. Wilson's voice growing fainter as he ascended the stairs, calling our softly and wheedlingly, "Here, kitty. Here, kitty,

kitty, kitty, kitty, kitty," and a few moments later Miss Hackman's joined in with a sugariness that made Carr shake:

"Here, kitty."

The voices moved off. Carr waited a little. Then he tiptoed across the room and peered through the bathroom door. The white-tiled cubicle was empty, but beyond it was another open door, leading to another bedroom.

He could see that it was a smaller bedroom, but friendlier. There was a littered dressing table with lamps whose little pink shades were awry. On the wall he recognized prints of paintings by Degas and Toulouse-Lautrec. Besides the dressing-table was a small bookcase overflowing with sheet-music piled helter-skelter and novels with bright, torn dust-covers. There was a bottle of ink on the dressing table, mixed in with the cosmetics. It was overturned and a large dry brown stain pooled out from it.

His heart began to pound as he crossed the bathroom's white tiles. He remembered the brown ink on the paper Jane had dropped.

But there was something strange about the bedroom he was approaching. Despite the lively, adolescent disorder, there was an ancient feel to it, almost a museum feel—like some historic room kept just as its illustrious occupant had left it. The novel on the dressing-table was last year's best seller.

Still . . .

He poked his hand through the door. Something moved beside him and he quickly turned his head.

He had only a moment to look before the blow fell. But in that moment, before the cap of pain was pulled down over his eyes and ears, blacking out everything, he recognized his assailant.

The cords in the neck stood out, the cheeks were drawn back, exposing the big front teeth, like those of a rat. Indeed the whole aspect—watery magnified eyes, low forehead, tangled dark hair, taut spindle-limbed figure—was that of a cornered rat.

It was the small dark man with glasses.

CHAPTER SEVEN

The Shimmering Garment

INCANDESCENT LIGHTS WERE shining in Carr's eyes, so bright they made his head ache violently. He jumped about in pain, flapping his arms. It seemed a stupid and degrading thing to be doing, even if he were in pain, so he tried to stop, he tried at least to use his hands to shield his eyes from the merciless light, but he couldn't. The reason was four ropes tied tight to his wrists and knees. The ropes went up into darkness overhead and were jerking him about, as if he were a puppet.

The ropes turned black, merged with the darkness, disappeared, and collapsed down into something soft and clinging.

Hitching himself up, he realized that he was in his own room, in his own bed, fighting the bedclothes.

He shakily thrust his feet out of bed and sat on the edge of it, waiting for the echoes of his nightmare to stop whirling through his senses, for his skin to loose its hot, tight, tingling feel.

His head ached miserably. Lifting his hand, he felt a large sensitive lump. He recalled the small dark man hitting him.

Pale light was sifting through the window. He got up, went over to the bureau, opened the top drawer. He looked at the three pint bottles of whisky. He chose the quarter full one, poured himself a drink, downed it, poured another, looked around.

The clothes he had been wearing were uncharacteristically laid out on a chair.

His head began to feel like a whirlpool. He went over and looked out the windows.

But instead of an empty street, open bedroom windows, flapping shades, and the other insignia of dawn, Carr saw a brisk little throng moving along the sidewalks. Windows were mostly lighted and advertisements were blinking. Unwillingly he decided that he must have been unconscious not only last night, but also all of to-day.

A coolness on his fingers told him that whisky was dribbling out of the shot glass. He drank it and turned around. A gust of anger at the small dark (is your friend!) went through him.

Just then he noticed a blank envelope propped up on the mantlepiece. He took it down, snapped on a light, opened it, unfolded the closely scribbled note it contained. It was from Jane.

I'm sorry about last night. Fred is sorry too, now that he knows who you are. He was hiding in my bedroom and he heard the others come in, and he thought you were one of them when you came sneaking through.

Don't try to find me, Carr. It isn't only that you'd risk your own life. You'd endanger mine. Fred and I are up against an organization that can't be beaten, only hidden from. If you try to find me, you'll only spoil my chances.

You want to have a long happy life, get married, be successful, don't you? You don't want your future changed, so that you have only a few wretched months or hours ahead of you, before you're hunted down? Then your only chance is to do what I tell you.

Stay in your room all day. Then arrange your things *just as you usually do* before going to work in the morning. You must be *very exact*—a lot depends on it. *Above all, burn this letter*—on your honor do that. Then dissolve in a glass of water the powders you'll find on the table beside your bed, and drink them. In a little while you'll go to sleep and when you wake up, everything will be all right.

Your only chance to get clear of the danger you're in, and to help me, is to do exactly as I've told you. And forget me forever.

Carr walked to the bed. On the little table, leaning against an empty tumbler, were two slim paper packets. He felt one between finger and thumb. It gritted. He put it back.

He glanced again at the letter. His head began to

ache stabbingly. Why, what sort of a nincompoop did they think he was? And what would she be saying next —"So sorry we had to poison you?" "Don't try to find me . . . burn this . . . on your honor . . . forget me forever . . ." What nauseous melodrama! Did she think such cheap phrases would soothe him into putting up with what had happened? Yes, she was romantic, all right—the romantic little dear who throws her arms around you and rubs her belly against yours so her boyfriend can stick a gun in your ribs.

He'd blundered into a pretty nasty affair, and maybe he'd picked the wrong side.

And she *did* have a reason to lie. She might lie to scare him off, to keep him from discovering what sort of hanky-panky she and her precious small dark man with glasses were up to, maybe to gain time for some sort of getaway. (Don't stir out of your room today.)

He hurriedly began to throw on his clothes, wincing when the jabs of pain came. After shouldering into his topcoat, he drained the last shot from the whisky bottle, tossed it back in the drawer, looked at the full bottles a moment, stuck one in his pocket, went out, glaring savagely at the mirror-imprisoned Carr on the stairs.

He walked a half block to the nearest hotel and waited for a cab. Two cruised by with their flags up, but the drivers ignored his arm-wavings and calls. He ground his teeth. Then a third cab approached and this one drew into the curb, but just as he was getting ready to board it, two fur-coated blondes from the hotel swept by him and piled in. He swore out loud, turned on his heel and started walking.

It was a pleasantly mild evening and he detested it. He felt a senseless rage at the people he passed.

How nice it would be to smash all the neon signs, rip down the posters, break into the houses and toss out of the windows the crooning, moaning, blatting radios and televisions. Come the atom bomb!

But for all that, the fresh air was helping his head. As he neared Mayberry Street, he began to calm down, or at least focus his anger.

Halfway down the block a car was parked with its motor softly chugging—a convertible with the top down. Just as he passed it, he saw a man come out of the entry to the Gregg apartment. A rather heavily built man.

72

He strolled off in the opposite direction. But before he turned, Carr had recognized him. Mr. Wilson!

Repressing the apprehension that surged through him, Carr made a snap decision. Stepping rapidly and decisively, he started after Mr. Wilson.

But just then a voice behind him said, "If you value your life or your reason, keep away from that guy." At the same time a hand gripped his elbow and spun him around.

This time the small dark man with glasses was wearing a black, snap-brim hat and a tightly buttoned trench coat rather too long for him, suggesting a robe. And this time he didn't look terrified, in spite of his pallor. Instead he was sardonically smiling.

"I knew you wouldn't stay in your room," he said. "I told Jane her letter would have just the opposite effect."

Carr doubled his fist, swung back his arm, hesitated. Damn it, he *did* wear glasses—pitifully thick-lensed ones.

"Go ahead," said the small, dark man. "Make a scene. Bring them down on us. I'm past caring."

And then he did something astonishing. He threw back his head and raised his arm in a theatrical gesture, and with a certain rakish coolness intoned, "If if be now, 'tis not to come; if it be not to come, it will be now; if it be not now, yet it will come; the readiness is all."

Carr stared at the glasses bright with reflected street light.

"Hamlet," said the small dark man. "Act five, scene two. The first quotation was from *The Hound of the Baskervilles*." He paused and studied Carr, his glasses gleaming hypnotically. "You wouldn't think, would you," he mused, "that as we stand here in this respectable neighborhood, conversing quietly, that we are both in deadly peril." He smiled. "No, I'm sure you wouldn't think that."

"Listen," said Carr suddenly, advancing again with baled fist. "You slugged me last night."

"So I did," said the small man, rocking on his heels.

"Well, in that case—" Carr started, and then he remembered Mr. Wilson. He whirled around. The portly man was nowhere in sight. He took a few steps, then checked himself abruptly, looked back. The small dark man was rapidly walking toward the purring converti-

73

ble. Carr darted after him, sprang to the running board just as the other slipped behind the wheel.

"You wanted to distract me until he was gone," Carr accused.

"That's right," said the small dark man. "Jump in."

Angrily Carr complied. But before he could say anything, the other had started to talk. His voice was no longer facetious, but low, bitter, almost confessional. His head was bent. He did not look at Carr.

"In the first place," he said, "I want you to understand that I don't trust you. And I certainly don't like you—if I did, I'd be doing my best to get you out of this instead of leading you straight toward the center. And finally, I don't give a damn what happens to you, or to myself. But I still do have a certain quixotic concern for what happens to Jane. It's for her sake, not yours, that I'm going to do what I'm going to do." He put his hand on the gear-shift lever.

"And what are you going to do?" snapped Carr. The convertible bucked, leaped forward with a roar.

Carr's gaze swung up as the grimy red wall of a truck loomed higher, higher. WORLD MOVERS, the sign said. He closed his eyes. He felt a blood-checking swerve, gritted his teeth at the wood-on-steel caress along their fender. When he opened his eyes again, it was to see a woman and child flash by not a foot from the wheels. He lurched sideways as they screamed around a corner, let go his hat to cling to the car, watched a coupe and bus converge ahead of them closed his eyes again as they grazed through the gap.

He wasn't going to die because of any mysterious, intrigue-sprawned peril. Oh, no! He and the small dark man with glasses were merely going to provide two unusually well-mangled additions to the year's traffic fatalities.

"Stop, you jerk!"

The other did not take his eyes off the street ahead, but bared his gums in a grin. Crouching there so small and frail behind the wheel, black hat blown off, hair streaming back, face contorted, peering ahead through glasses thick as telescope lenses, he looked like some spindle-bodied man of the future hurling himself at eternity.

To either side, small indistinguishable stores and

dusty white street globes shot by, while blocks of asphalt vanished under the hood.

"Tell me what it's all about before you kill us," yelled Carr.

The small dark man snickered through his teeth. "Do I dare explain the universe?"

Ahead of them cars skittered to the curb like disturbed ants. Over the motor's roar Carr became aware of a wailing that grew in volume. A wild white light, mixed with red, began to flood the street from behind them, its beam swinging back and forth like a giant pendulum. Then from the corner of his eye Carr noticed a seated man in a big black slicker, traveling at a level several feet above him, heave into view, creep abreast. Below and ahead of the man was a bright vermillion hood from which the wailing came. Behind man and hood were dim ladders and coils, other swaying and slickered figures.

Ahead the street took a jog. Cars parked zigzag like a rail fence made it impossible that both their car and the fire engine should get through.

Grinning wider, the small dark man nursed the throttle. The fire engine dropped back a little, hung on tenaciously, dropped back just enough more to let them careen through the gap, while frozen pedestrians gaped.

Carr's fear left him. There was no use to it.

"You and Jane are both insane, aren't you?" he screamed.

The small man's snort seemed to be torn from his lips by the wind.

"That would be nice," he said.

The street narrowed, its sides grew dark. Behind them the fire engine braked, took a turn.

From ahead came a cold whiff of water and oil. Skyscrapers twinkled against the sky, but just this side of them a gap in the buildings was widening. Immediately ahead a skeletal black structure loomed.

A rapid clanging started. Towers flanking the black structure began to blink red.

Without warning Carr grabbed for the ignition, stamped at the brake. "They're opening the bridge!" he yelled.

The small man kicked him in the ankle, punched his hand away from the dashboard and accelerated. Ahead were stopped autos, the black-and-white semaphore of a barrier. Swinging far to the left, they struck its flexible end. It rasped along the car's side like a stick against a picket fence, tore free with a great twang. They shot forward onto the dark span. To either side, solidity dropped away. Far below, yellow windows of sky-scrapers flowed in uneven patterns on the water. To the left was the dark bulk of a lake freighter with figures moving on the dimly lit bridge. Beside it Carr seemed to glimpse a much smaller hull and the tiny pale oval of a single upturned face.

They were three-quarters of the way across when, through their hurtling speed, Carr felt the feather touch of a titan. Under them the span had begun to rise. Ahead of them a ribbon of blackness appeared, at the break in the jack-knife of the span.

The small dark man clamped the throttle to the floor. There was a spine-compressing jar and jounce, the sky-scrapers reeled, then another jar, as the car came down—on its wheels.

The tip of the second barrier broke off with a giant snap. The open bridge had cleared the street ahead of traffic going their way. The small dark man breezed along it for four blocks like the winner of a race, then suddenly braked, skidded around a corner to the wrong side of the street. The two wheels on his side hit the curb and the car rocked to a stop.

Carr loosened his death-grip on dashboard and door-handle, balled a fist, and turned, this time without any compunction about glasses.

But the small man had jumped out of the car and was lightly running up the steps of a building that Carr now realized was the public library. As he hit the sidewalk in pursuit, he saw the small man briefly silhouetted against the yellow rectangle of a swinging door. When Carr stiff-armed through it, the man was vanishing at the top of a flight of marble stairs, under an archway decorated in twinkling gold mosaic with the names of Whittier, Emerson and Longfellow.

Reaching the top, Carr received a spurt of savage pleasure from the realization that he was gaining. Before him was a large, domed room, open shelves to one side, counters and booths to the other, unoccupied except for a couple of girls behind a window and a baldheaded man with a coat and briefcase awkwardly clamped under one arm as he stood on tiptoe to reach down a book.

The small dark man was racing under an archway commemorating the English poets Scott, Burns, Tennyson and Gray.

Carr raced at his heels past a desk behind which sat a starved, grayhaired woman who seemed too timid to look up or too fragile to permit herself quick reflexes. The small man darted toward a wall bearing long golden characters and Egyptian hieroglyphs. He ducked down a narrow corridor and to his shock Carr realized they were both running on frosted glass.

For a moment Carr thought that the small dark man had led him this long chase solely to get him to step through a skylight. Then he realized that he was on one of the many translucent catwalks that served as aisles in the stacks of the library. He sprinted forward again, guided by the sonorous pit-pat of receding footsteps.

He found himself in a silent world within a world. A world several stories high and covering a good part of a block. An oddly insubstantial world of thin metal beams, narrow stairs, translucent runways, and innumerable books. A world of crannies, slits and gaps.

Thus far, Carr had gained. But now, like some animal that has reached its native element, the small dark man held his own, craftily doubling and redoubling on his course, suddenly darting up or down stairs whose treads resounded like the clangor of ancient war. Carr caught glimpses of a flapping raincoat, he shook his fist with anger at some teeth and a grin spied through castellated gaps in successive tiers of books, he clutched futilely at a small, expensive-looking oxford disappearing up a metal-treaded stair in a tantalizing leisurely fashion.

He was panting and his side had begun to hurt, something in his topcoat was growing heavier. It began to seem to him that the chase would never end, that the two of them would go skipping and staggering on indefinitely, always the same distance apart. The whole experience had acquired nightmarish overtones. They were rats scampering through the fact-walled convolutions of some giant metal brain of the far future. They were human specimens awakened too soon in a gigantic time-capsule and frantically seeking escape.

Carr lurched around a corner and there, not ten feet away, back turned, standing beside an old-brass-fitted drinking fountain that gurgled merrily, was his quarry.

Carr almost hiccuped a laugh between his gasps for air. Now, Carr decided, he'd slug the guy.

As he moved forward, however, it was inevitable that he should look beyond the small dark man at the thing at which the small dark man was looking.

Or rather, the person.

For just inside the next alleyway, gilt-buttoned brown suit almost exactly the same shade as the buckram bindings that made a background, lips formed in an ellipse of dismay that couldn't avoid becoming a smile, stood Jane.

Carr found himself drifting past the small dark man as if the latter were part of a dissolving dream. With every step forward the floor seemed to get solider under his feet.

Jane's expression did not change and her lips held the same shape. She just tilted her head as he put his arms around her and kissed her.

"Real, real, real," was the only thought in his head. Real as the *Masters of the Chessboard*, R. RETI, just beyond her hair, or *My System*, NIMZOWITCH, beside it.

She pushed away, looking up at him incredulously. His nerves, soothed for a moment, reawoke with a jerk. He stepped back.

"Where's he gone?" he asked.

"Who?"

"The small dark madman with glasses." He moved about quickly, looking down all the nearby aisles.

"I don't know," she said. "He has a way of fading."

"I'll say he has!" He turned on her. "Though generally he tries to murder you first."

"What!"

"Maybe he thought we had a suicide pact." Carr grinned woodenly as he said it, but his hands were shaking. He could feel all his delayed reactions to the ride, to his painful awakening earlier, to her exasperating note—coming to the surface.

"Jane," he said sharply, "what's it all about?"

She backed away from him, shaking her head.

He followed her. His voice was harsh. "Look, Jane,"

he said. "Day before yesterday your boy friend ran away from me. Last night he knocked me out. Tonight he tried to kill both of us. What's it all about? I want to know."

She made no answer. The fear in her eyes brought his exasperation to a boil. "What have you and he done? Who are those people after you? What's wrong with your father and mother? Why did you lead me to that empty house? What are you doing here? You've got to tell me, Jane! You've got to!"

He had her backed up against the bookshelves and was almost shouting in her face. But she would only stare up at him terrifiedly and shake her head. His control snapped. He grabbed her by the shoulders and shook her violently.

It was a paroxysm of exasperation. He felt as if he were shaking the last two days, with all their enigmas and frustrations. This floppy brown doll in his arms somehow stood for the small man, his car, Miss Hackman, Mr. Wilson, the man with one hand, the whole bedeviled city of Chicago.

But no matter how violently her head snapped back and forth, her lips remained pressed tightly together. Suddenly he loosed her and turned away, resting his elbows on a shelf, burying his face in his hands, breathing heavily.

When he looked up and around she was still backed up against the shelves, smoothing her suit. She bit her lip when her hand touched her shoulder. She was looking at him. "Do I shake well?" she asked. "You know, it's rather relaxing."

He winced. "Sorry," he said dully. "I'm acting crazy. But I've just got to know."

"I can't tell you."

He looked at her in a misery of exasperation. "Jane!"

"No, I can't."

He submitted wearily. "All right. But . . ." He glanced around vaguely. "We've got to get out of here!" he said, jumping away from the shelves against which he'd been leaning.

"Why?" She was as uncomprehending as before, and much cooler.

"We're in the stacks." His voice automatically took on a hushed tone. "No one can come here without a

79

pass. We made enough racket to wake the dead. They're bound to come looking for us."

"Are they?" She smiled. "They haven't yet."

"And then—Good Lord!—the traffic cops and who knows who else . . . they're bound to!" He looked down the long aisles apprehensively.

She smiled again. "But they haven't."

Carr turned wondering eyes on her. Something of the charming willfulness of the night before last seemed to have returned to her. Carr felt an answering spirit rising in himself.

And it did seem the height of silliness to worry about being caught breaking library regulations just after you'd escaped messy death a dozen times.

"All right," he said. "In that case let's have a drink." And he fished out of his pocket the unopened pint of whisky.

"Swell," she said, her eyes brightening. "The fountain's right here. I'll get paper cups."

Carr lowered his cup, half emptied.

"Listen," he said. "There's someone coming."

He hustled Jane to the next aisle, which was unlighted.

The footsteps grew louder, ringing on the glass.

"Let's go farther back," Carr whispered. "He might see us here."

But Jane refused to budge. He peered over her shoulder. "Damn!" he breathed. "I forgot the bottle. He's bound to spot it."

Jane's shoulders twitched.

The he turned out to be a she, as Carr saw by patches through the gaps between the shelves. And a rather remarkable she, with a large, child-of-the-theater face, sleek long black hair cut in bangs across the forehead, and a tight, dark red dress. She walked staccato with a swish.

And she was making faces. Here in the privacy of the stacks, her face—surely it had been composed in childlike dignity back at the counters—was running a remarkable gamut: hatred, horror, smiling contempt, agonized grief, an idiot's glee, tragic resignation, the magnetism of sex. And not just such fleeting expressions as any neurotic might let slip, but good full-blooded ones, worthy of some cruel Russian princess pacing in

her bed-chamber as she contemplated an elaborate revenge against all her seventeen unfaithful lovers.

The expressions succeeded one another regularly,
without pause. They looked to Carr rather like an exercise in acting.

The girl walked past their alley, stopped at the second one beyond. She looked up.

"Here we are, boys and girls," they heard her say to
herself in a loud, better voice. "Oh, in six volumes, is
it? Is that all he expects at closing time?" She scribbled
briefly on a slip of paper she was carrying. "Sorry,
Baldy, but—out! You'll have to learn about the secrets
of sex some other day."

And making a final face, apparently straight at Jane
and Carr, she returned the way she had come.

Carr recovered the bottle. "Do you suppose she
thought we were doing research work?"

Jane said lightly, "She looked tolerant."

She went into the next aisle and returned with a
couple of stools. Carr pushed his trenchcoat back over
some books. He chuckled. "That was quite an act she
put on."

"All people do that," Jane said seriously. "As soon
as the door closes and they know they're alone, they
begin to act out a little drama. Each person has his
own, which he's made up. It may be love, fear, hate—
anything. Sometimes it's very broad and melodramatic
or farcical, sometimes it's extremely subtle and restrained.
But everyone has one."

"How can you know," Carr asked, half humorously,
"if they only do it when they're sure they're alone?"

"I know," said Jane simply. For a moment they were
silent. Then Jane moved nervously. "Let's have another
drink."

Carr filled their cups. It was rather shadowy where
they were. Jane reached up and tugged a cord. Light
spilled around them. There was another pause.

Carr said, "Well, since you won't tell me about yourself yet . . ." He made it half a question; she shook her
head, turning away, ". . . I have something to tell you."
And he told her how he had spied on Miss Hackman
and Mr. Wilson at General Employment and in the
tobacco store.

That captured her attention, all right. She sat tensely.
"You're sure they didn't spot you?" she pressed when

81

he was done. "You're sure she meant it when she said she'd found nothing suspicious?"

"As sure as can be," he told her, "knowing as little as I do. Anyway, I was bothered and I wanted to warn you. I went to the place where I'd left you the night before. Of course, it knocked me for a loop to see a 'for sale' sign, but then by the merest luck I found a paper you'd dropped, which happened to have your right address on it . . ."

"I know."

"How?" He looked at her.

She hesitated. Then, "Because I was watching you," she admitted, dropping her eyes. "I hadn't intended to tell you that."

"You were *watching* me?"

"Yes. I thought you might go back there, trying to find me again, and I was worried."

"But where were you?" He still hardly believed her.

"Inside. Watching through a crack in one of those boarded-up windows. I found a way in."

He stared at her. "But if you came back on my account, why didn't you come out when you saw me?"

"Oh, I didn't want you to *find* me," she explained naively. "I'm doing my best to keep you out of this, though I know it doesn't exactly look that way. I'm afraid there's an unscrupulous part of my mind that's working against me and keeps trying to draw you in." Again she looked down. "I suppose it was that part of my mind that made me accidentally drop the envelope with the address where you'd remember it. And before that, write that silly note about the lion's tail and the five sisters."

He looked at her a while longer. Then, with an uncomprehending sigh, he continued, "So I went over to your place."

"I know," she interrupted. "I followed you."

He dropped his hands on his knees, leaned forward. "And still you didn't—?"

"Oh, no," she assured him. "I didn't want you to see me. I was just anxious."

"But then you must know all the rest," he expostulated. "How I finally went upstairs and how Miss Hackman and Mr. Wilson came and . . ."

"Yes," she said. "As soon as that happened I ran

around and went up the back stairs. I found Fred and you . . ."

"Fred?"

"The small dark man with glasses. I found you in the bedroom. He'd just hit you. Miss Hackman and Mr. Wilson were killing Gigolo in the front hall . . ."

"Your cat?"

She shut her eyes. "Yes." She went on after a moment. "I told Fred who you were and we carried you down the back way to his car and . . ."

"Wait a minute," he said. "How did your friend Fred happen to be there in the first place? I got the impression you hadn't been in that room of yours for months."

"Oh," she said uncomfortably, "Fred has very queer habits, a sort of morbid sentimentality about me. He often goes to my room, though I'm never there. Don't ask me any more about that now."

"All right, so you carried me down to your car," he said. "Then—?"

"We found your address in your pocketbook and drove you back to your room and carried you up, using your key and put you to bed. I was worried about you, I wanted to stay though I know I shouldn't, but Fred said you'd be all right, so . . ."

". . . you departed," he finished for her, "after writing me this charming little note." And he fished it out of his pocket.

"I asked you to burn that," she said.

"How do you suppose I felt, waking up?" he asked her. "Happy about it all? Oh yes, and you left those powders too—no, I didn't bring them with me—those powders I was supposed to swallow so trustfully . . ."

"You should have," she cut in. "Really you should have. Don't you see, Carr, I'm trying to keep you out of this? If you only knew what I'd give to be in a position where I could still keep out of it." She broke off.

He refused to be moved by the intensity of feeling she had revealed. "You've talked a lot about 'this,' Jane," he said deliberately, leaning back. She looked at him frightenedly. "Now it's time you really told me something," he continued. "Just what is 'this'?"

A bell clanged. They both started.

She relaxed. "Closing time," she explained.

Carr shrugged. The fact that they were in the stacks of the Chicago Public Library had become inconsequential to him. "Just what is 'this'?" he started to repeat.

"How did you get down here tonight?" she interrupted quickly, looking away.

"All right," he said, meaning that he was patient and his own question could wait. He refilled both their cups. Then, without hurrying, he told her about going back to the apartment on Mayberry and meeting Fred. Revisualizing the ride shook him, though its details were beginning to seem incredible.

And it seemed to shake Jane too. Though when he finished he realized it was anger which was making her tremble.

"Oh, the coward," she breathed. "The awful coward. Pretending to be gallant, pretending to sacrifice his own feelings, even to the point of bringing you to me—but really just doing it to hurt me, because he knew I had done my best to keep you out of this. And then on top of it all, taking chances with your life, hoping that you would both die while he was being noble!" Her lips curled. "No, he doesn't love me any more, unless morbidness and self-torment count for love. I don't think he ever did."

"But why do you go with him then?"

"I don't, she replied unhappily. "Except that he's the only person in the whole world to whom I can go and . . ." Again she broke off.

"Are you sure of that, Jane?" His voice was low. His hand touched her sleeve.

She pulled her arm away. "Why don't you go away, Carr?" she pleaded, eying him with a kind of wild fright. "Why don't you drink the powders and forget? I don't want to drag you down. You've got a job and a woman and a life, a path through the world laid out for you. You don't have to walk into the darkness, the meaninglessness, the chaos, the black machine."

The lights in the stacks began to wink off, all but the one above their heads.

"Another drink?" she asked in a small voice.

There wasn't much left in the bottle when he'd filled the cups. She accepted hers absently, looking beyond him. Her face seemed incredibly tiny now, as she sat hunched on her stool, her brown suit shading into the background. The stacks were silent; the mutter of the city was inaudible. In all directions the aisles stretched off into darkness, from their single light. All around them was the pressure of the hundreds of thousands of books. But always the gaps between the books, the tunneling slits, the peepholes.

"Look at it from my point of view, Jane," Carr said, "Just how maddening it seems. I know you're running away from something horrible. Fred is, too. I know there's some kind of organization I never dreamed of loose in the world, and that it's threatening you. I know there's something terribly wrong with your parents. But what? I can't even make a guess. I've tried to make things fit together, but they won't. Just think, Jane—you coming to me in terror . . . that slap right out in the open . . . your warning . . . Miss Hackman searching my desk . . . the words I overheard about 'checking on you' and 'having fun' . . ." Jane shuddered. He went on, "Those crazy notes you'd made on the envelope . . . the queer piano in your folks' place . . . your mother crazily pretending you were there or whatever it was . . . your father humoring her, or crazily pretending to . . . Miss Hackman and Mr. Wilson busting in, ignoring them, acting as if they weren't alive . . . more talk about 'checking' and 'fun' and a 'beast' and some sort of threatening 'other groups'—all the while acting as if the rest of humanity were beneath contempt . . . and then the cat . . . and Fred almost killing me . . . and his wild, fatuous talk tonight about 'deadly peril' and so on . . . and that insane ride . . . and now you hiding here in the stacks of the Chicago Public Library . . ."

He shook his head hopelessly.

"They just won't fit into any pattern, no matter how crazy." He hesitated. "And then two or three times," he went on, frowning, "I've had the feeling that the explanation was something utterly inconceivable, something far bigger, more dreadful—"

"Don't," she interrupted. "Don't ever let yourself start thinking about it that way."

"At any rate, don't you see why you've *got* to tell me about it, Jane?" he finished.

For a moment there was silence. Then she said, "If I tell you about it, that is, if I tell you partly about it, will you promise to go and do what I asked you in the note? So you can escape?"

"No. I won't promise anything until after you've told me."

There was another silence. Then she sighed, "All right, I'll tell you partly. But always remember that you made me do it!" She paused, then began, "About a year-and-a-half ago I met Fred. There was nothing serious between us. We just used to meet in the park and go for walks. My father and mother didn't know about him. I used to spend most of the time working at the piano, and I was going to music school. I didn't know then that those three—Miss Hackman and Mr. Wilson and Dris— were after Fred. He hadn't told me anything. But then one day they saw us together. And because of that, because those three had linked me with Fred, my life was no longer safe. I had to run away from home. Since then I've lived as I could, here, there, I've tried to be inconspicuous, I've made notes to remind me what I must and mustn't do, I've stayed in places like this, talked to no one, slept in parks, empty apartments . . ."

"But that's impossible."

"It's true. For a time I managed to escape them. Then a week ago they started to close in on me. When I went to your office I was desperate. I went there because someone I knew long ago worked there . . ."

"Tom Elvested?"

"Don't interrupt. But then I saw you, I saw you weren't busy and I went to you. I knew it was my last chance. And you helped me, you pretended . . ." She hesitated. "That's all," she finished.

"Oh, Jane," Carr said, after a moment, as one might say to a schoolchild who hasn't prepared her lesson, "you haven't told me anything. What—" But his voice lacked its former insistence. He was getting tired now, tired of pushing things, of straining after facts. He wanted . . . He hardly knew what he wanted. He divided the rest of the liquor between them, but it was hardly more than a sip. "Look, Jane," he said, making a last weary effort, "won't you trust me? Won't you stop being so frightened? I do want to help you."

She looked at him, not quite smiling. "You've been awfully nice to me, Carr," she said. "You've given me courage and a little forgetfulness—the Custer's Last Stand bar, the music store, the movie, the chess, the touching by the gate. I've been pretty rotten to you. I've made use of you, exposed you to dangers, left you

86

hurt, dragged you back by unconscious tricks into my private underworld. If you knew the real situation, I think you'd understand. But that's something I'll have to battle out myself. It's honestly true what I wrote you in that note, Carr. You can't help me, you can only spoil my chance of escape." She looked down. "It isn't because I think you can help me that I keep drawing you back," she added, and paused.

"There are two kinds of people in the world, Carr. The steadies and the waifs. The steady knows where he and the world are going. The waif sees only darkness. She knows a secret about life that locks her away forever from happiness and rest. You're really a steady, Carr. That woman you told me about who wants you to succeed, she's a steady too. It's no use helping a waif, Carr. No matter how tender-hearted she may be, how filled with good intentions, there's something destructive about her, something akin to the darkness, something that makes her want to destroy other people's certainties and faiths, lead them to the precipice and then point down and say, 'See? Nothing!' And there's nothing you can do for me, nothing at all."

Carr shook his head. "I *can* help," he persisted.

"No."

"Oh, but Jane, don't you understand? I really want to help you." He started to put his arm around her, but she quickly got up.

"What's the matter?" he asked, following her.

She turned, putting her hand between them. She had trouble speaking. "Go away, Carr. Go away right now. Go back to that wonderful new business you told me about and that woman who wants you to have it. Forget everything else. I thought it would be fun to be with you for an evening, to pretend that things were different —I was insane! Every minute you stay with me, I'm doing you a wrong. Please go, Carr."

"No."

"Then stay with me for a little while. Stay with me tonight, but go away tomorrow."

"No."

They stood facing each other tautly for a moment. Then the tension suddenly sagged. Carr rubbed his eyes and exclaimed, "Dammit, I wish I had a drink."

Jane's eyes suddenly twinkled. Carr sensed an abrupt change in her. She seemed to have dropped her cloak of fear and thrown around her shoulders another garment, which he couldn't identify, except that it shimmered. Even before she spoke, he felt his spirits rising in answer to hers.

"Since you won't recognize danger and go, let's forget it for tonight," was what she told him. "Only, you must promise one thing." Her eyes gleamed strangely. "You must believe that I am . . . magic, that I have magical powers, that while you are with me, you can do anything you want to in the world and it can't do anything to you, that you're free as an invisible spirit. You promise? Good. And now I believe you said you wanted a drink."

He followed her as if she were some fairy-tale princess as she went three aisles over, pulled on a light, took down from an upper shelf three copies of Walter Pater's *Marius the Epicurean,* stuck her hand into the gap, and brought out a fifth of scotch.

"I put it here two months ago," she said. "That was when I realized that solitary drinking was a bad thing." Suddenly she set the bottle down, shook him, cried, "You're risking your life by your stubbornness, do you understand that? What we're doing is horribly dangerous. I don't care, I want to, but still it's horribly dangerous. Do you understand?"

But his eyes were on the bottle of scotch. "Do you *live* down here?" he demanded.

She laughed helplessly and let go of him. "In a way. Would you like to see?" And recklessly pulling out handfuls of other books so that they thudded on the floor, she showed him a pack-rat accumulation of cosmetics, showy jewelry, bags of peanuts and candy, cans of gourmet food and an opener, boxes of crackers, loose handkerchiefs, gloves, scarves, all sorts of little boxes and bottles, cups, plates, and glasses.

Taking two of the latter, crystal, long-stemmed, she said, "And now will you have a drink with me, in my house?"

CHAPTER EIGHT

The Strip Tease

LIKE TWO DRUNKEN stowaways in the hold of a ship, tipsily swaying and constantly shushing each other, Carr and Jane ascended a narrow stair. They groped through the foreign language section, and surveyed the library's lightless rotunda. Carr's heart immediately went out to the shadows festooning it. They looked as warm and friendly as the scotch had tasted. He felt he could fly up to them if he willed, wrap them around him fold on fold, luxuriate in their smoky softness. Light from outside, slanting upward through the windows, evoked golden and greenish gleams from the mosaic. Lower down, shelves and counters made blurry-edged rectangles. The longer Carr looked, the more he rejoiced at the cosmetic magic of darkness.

They were halfway across the rotunda when a beam of light began to bob through the archway ahead. Carr pulled Jane toward the information booth.

"What's the matter?" she mumbled, resisting. "What are you doing?"

"The watchman!" he whispered urgently, dragging her along.

She said foolishly, "Who cares?"

"Shh!" He pulled her into the booth and down into a crouch beside him.

The light swam closer. The tread of rubber-shod feet became audible. The light swung around slowly, poking into the shadows. Once it swept across their hiding place, like an enemy searchlight over a foxhole, showing the grain in the oak counter just above Carr's head. And once it leaped to the ceiling and mystically spotlighted the golden name of Corneille.

A cracked voice began to hum softly, "I want, a girl just like the girl that married dear old Dad."

Jane started to peek over the counter. Carr managed

to pull her down noiselessly. In doing it, he glimpsed an old man half turned away from them, with a clock strapped to his belt.

Once again the light brushed across their retreat. Then it and the footsteps started away.

"He wants a girl," Jane whispered and giggled.

"Shh!"

"I won't unless you stop hurting my wrist."

"Shh!" Nevertheless he let go of her. A few seconds later he raised his head until his eyes were above the level of the counter, but just at that moment he heard Jane scramble over it at the other end of the booth. Forsaking caution, he gave a push at what he thought was the swinging door, smacked solid wood instead, and without bothering to hunt any further, vaulted after Jane.

Weaving behind her down the broad white stair, he felt the contagion of her recklessness. They might be prince and princess stealing from a marble castle, bound on some dangerous escapade.

Then Carr realized that Janes had got through the door to the street. He followed her and halted, entranced. For there, beyond the wide sidewalk, was a most fitting, even though anachronistic, continuation of his fantasy—a long low limousine with silvery fittings and softly glowing interior.

Then he saw that approaching it at a stately waddle came two well-fed couples in top hats and bright feathery capes. Under the street light, the features of all four were screwed up into that expression of germicidal abstraction which is the customary mask of the Four Hundred. While they were still some yards away, a chauffeur opened the door and touched his visored cap.

Jane had scampered down the stairs. Now Carr watched in growing amazement as she headed straight for the sedate waddlers, verred off at the very last moment, but in passing them reached out her hand and deliberately knocked off the nearest top hat. *And the old fool wearing it marched on without even turning his head.*

It hit Carr with all the instant impact of that crucial drink which opens the door to wonderland. It was as if his spirits had exploded like a fountain from his chest. There at his feet and Jane's lay the city—a playground, a zoo, a nursery, a congregation of lock-stepping fools, afraid to show any reaction, even to outrage. Their eyes glued on advertisements, their hands clutched on pocketbooks, their thoughts shuffling stupidly as devil-dancers around a monolith of infantile inhibitions and frustrations. It was just as Jane had told him! You could do anything! No one could stop you! You were free!

With a whoop he raised his arms and ran lurchingly across the sidewalk at a wide angle that caught him up with Jane so that they raced around the corner hand in hand.

And now they were prince and princess no longer, but wizard's children, sorcerer's apprentices with stolen cloaks of invisibility, charter members of some modern and magical Hellfire Club. Under their winged feet the pavements sped. Neon signs caressed their cheeks with ruby, topaz and sapphire. Motors and horns struck up a dulcet, nerve-quickening music, suitable for acrobats preparing their star turn.

Across their path a theatre lobby spilled a gabbling, cigarette-puffing, taxi-hailing horde. Oh, the beautiful joy of rushing through them, of jostling powdered shoulders, of hopelessly tangling half-donned overcoats, of plucking at ties and shawls under the glare of yellow light-banks, of bobbing up and gibbering like apes into faces too staid or startled to dare let on they saw you. Then spinning into the clear like broken-field runners, to lope for a half-lock that was empty but for a crouched, seeing-eye blind man, to sprinkle him with a handful of pennies, to hurtle into a band of stragglers from a 1925-rococo movie palace—the same den of shadows he and Jane had deserted for chess two evenings ago—and to serve them just as you'd served their wealthier co-fools down the block.

Next, in an exhibition of hair-raising daring and split-second dexterity, to spring from the sidewalk and dart between speeding cab and green sedan, to jeer at the drivers, almost to slip and sprawl on gleaming tracks in front of a vast rhinoceros of a streetcar, to regain balance deftly and glide between moving chromium bumpers just beyond, finally to gain the opposite sidewalk, your ears ringing with a great shout such as might have greeted Blondin on his first tight-wire crossing of Niagara Falls —and to realize that you had uttered that shout yourself!

Oh, to hiss into the ear of a fat woman with smug suburban face, "The Supreme Court has just declared soap-operas unconstitutional," to scream at a solemn man with eleven-dollar shirt, "The Democrats have set up a guillotine in Grant Park!" to say to a mincing, dopey-eyed sweater girl, "I'm a talent scout. Follow me," to a well-dressed individual with an aura of superiority, "Gallup Poll. Do you approve of Charlemagne's policies toward the Saxons?" to a slinking clerk, "Burlesque is back," to a hod-carrier, "Free beer behind the booths, ask for Clancy," to a fish-faced bookie, "Here, hold my pocket-book," to a slim intellectual with a brief case, at court-stenographer speed, "'Watch the sky. A wall of atomic catastrophe, ignited by injudicious Sweedish experiments, is advancing across Labrador, great circle route, at the rate of seventeen hundred and ninety-seven miles an hour."

And finally, panting, sides needled by delicious breathlessness, to sink to the curb near a busy intersection and sit with back resting against metal trash box and laugh and laugh, gaspingly, in each other's faces, doubling up after each new glimpse of the hustling crowd on the conveyor-belt called a sidewalk, every single face too proper or blasé-blind to look at you— and the equally wooden visages behind the wheels of the endless stop-starting striing of cars that almost pinched your toes as they went grunting by.

Just then a police siren sounded and a large gray truck grumbled to a stop in front of them. Without hesitation, Carr scooped up Jane and sat her on the projecting backboard, then scrambled up beside her.

The light changed and they jounced across the intersection. The siren's wail rose in volume and pitch as a paddy wagon turned into their street a block behind them. It swung far to the left, around a whole string of cars, and careened into a pocket just behind them. They looked into the eyes of two red-jowled coppers. Jane thumbed her nose at them.

The paddy wagon braked to a stop at the curb and several policemen poured out of it and into a dingy hotel.

"Won't find us there," smirked Carr. "We're high-class." Jane squeezed his hand.

The truck passed under the dark steel canopy of the Elevated. Its motor growled as it labored up the approach to the bridge.

"I've a private barge on the river," said Carr airily.

"Unpretentious, but homey. And a most intellectual bargeman. Physical and mental giant. He'll carry us to the ports of Hell and back and talk philosophy with us all the way."

"Not tonight," said Jane.

Carr pointed at the splintered end of the barrier. "Your friend did that on his way down," he informed her amiably. "I wish he were along with us." He looked at Jane. "No, I don't," he added.

"Neither do I," she told him.

His face was close to hers, he started to put his arms around her, but a sudden rush of animal spirits caused him instead to plant his palms on the backboard and lift himself up, feet kicking.

He fell backward into the truck as Jane yanked at him. "You're still quite breakable, you know," she told him and kissed him and sat up quickly.

As he struggled up beside her, the truck hustled down the worn brick incline at the opposite end of the bridge and ground to a stop. A maroon and green awning stretched to the edge of the sidewalk. Above the awning, backed by ancient windows painted black, a bold, blinking, blue neon script proclaimed: *Goldie's Casablanca*.

"That's us," said Carr. He hopped down and lifted Jane off as the truck started up again.

Inside the solid glass door beneath the awning, a tall, tuxedo-splitting individual with the vacant smile of a one-time sparring partner, was remonstrating quietly with an arm-swinging fat man whom he held pinned against the wall with one hand. Jane and Carr swept past them. Carr whipped out several dollar bills and held them clipped between bent finger and thumb. They descended a short flight of stairs, made a sharp turn, and found themselves in the noisiest and most crowded night-club in the world.

The bar, which ran along the wall to their left, was jammed three deep. Behind it towered two horse-faced men in white coats. The one was reaching behind him for a bottle. The other was violently shaking a silver cylinder above his head, but the rattle was lost in the general din. He might, Carr thought, be performing a mysterious rite in honor of the Moorish maidens on the mural behind him. The willowy harem figures suggested El Greco, but someone—Goldie no doubt—had pasted cut-out, larger-than-life-size photographs of the faces of popular movie stars just above their bright yellow necks. The effect was arresting.

Packed tables, with no discernible aisles between, extended from the foot of the stairs to the edge of a small and slightly raised dance floor, upon which, like some thick vegetable stew being stirred by the laziest cook in creation, a solid mass of hunchedly embracing couples was slowly revolving.

The tinkly music for this elephantine exercise, almost as inaudible as the cocktail shaker, came from somewhere behind an inward-facing phalanx of alternately black and bare shoulders toward the far end of the wall to the right.

Everyone, even the dancers, seemed to be talking as fast as they could get the words out and as forcefully as the strength of tobacco-fogged lungs would permit.

Two couples marched straight at Carr. He swung aside, bumping a waiter who was coming around the end of the bar with a tray of cocktails. The waiter checked himself while the others passed, a crashing chord jetted up over the phalanx, applause vehement as carpet-beating began, and Carr substituted two of the bills for two of the cocktails just as the waiter continued forward and another couple came between them. Deftly holding the two cocktails in one hand and the rest of the bills in the other, Carr turned to Jane. But she had already left him and was edging through the press some tables away. Beyond her was a busy door marked "Setters," close beside another labeled "Pointers." Carr grimaced, leaned against the wall, closed his eyes, downed one of the cocktails, put the empty glass in his pocket and slowly sipped the other.

When he opened his eyes again, the dancers had all squeezed themselves into hitherto imperceptible nooks and crannies around the tables. The phalanx had dispersed to reveal a grossly fat man whose paunch abutted the keyboard of a tiny, cream-colored piano. A short apish individual who looked all dazzling white shirtfront—Goldie, surely at last—was standing on the edge of the empty dance floor and saying in a loud hoarse voice that in total lack of any honest enthusiasm would have been very suitable for a carp: "And now let's give the little chick a great big ovation!"

The earnest carpet-beaters started to work again.

Goldie, ducking down from the platform, rewarded them with a cold sneer. The fat man's hands began to scuttle up and down the keyboard like two fat white rats. And a blonde in a small black dress stepped up on the platform. She held in one hand something that might have been a shabby muff.

But even as the applause swelled, most of the people at the tables started to jabber at each other again.

Carr shivered. Here you have it, he thought suddenly —the bare stage, the unlistening audience, the ritual of the machine. The bacchanal shrunk to a precalculated and profit-motivated booze-fest under the direction of a Pan who'd gone all to watery flesh and been hitting the dope for two thousand years. The dreadful rhythm of progress without purpose. Did these people see or hear at all? Did they taste or touch? Did they even thrill to their drunkenness? Oh, into what sterile corners the whip of beauty-hunger has driven the drugged, near-dead if not dead already, spirit of man!

The blonde raised her arm and the muff unfolded to show, capping her unseen hand, a small face of painted wood that was at once foolish, frightened and lecherous. Two diminutive hands flapped beside it. The blonde began to hum to the music.

Continuing to toy with the piano, the fat man glanced around briefly. In a rapid, piping voice on the verge of a titter he confided, "And now you shall hear the sad tale of that most unfortunate creature, Peter Puppet."

Carr finished his second drink in a gulp, looked around for Jane, couldn't see her.

"Peter was a perfect puppet," the fat man intoned leisurely, accompanying himself with suitable runs and chords. Carr leaned forward, frowning. It was hard to hear with the jabber going on. "Yes, Peter was the prize Pinocchio of them all. He was carved out of wood to resemble a human being in complete detail, oh the most complete detail. Peter had everything a man has . . . in wood!"

The puppet made eyes at the blonde. She ignored him and began to dance sketchily.

The fat man whirled on tables, beetling his brows, "But he had one fault!" he half-shrieked. "He wanted to be alive!" Then, going back to the lazy titter, "Yes, our Peter wanted to be a man. He wanted to do everything a man does. He even wanted to do those things

95

that you'd never, never, never think could be done by a gentleman . . . with wooden parts!"

Some guffaws came through the general jabber. The fat man's hands darted venomously along the keyboard, eliciting dreamy, pastoral tones.

"Then one lovely spring day while Peter was wandering through the meadows, wishing he were a man, he chanced to see a beautiful, a simply be-unbelievably be-yutiful be-londe. Peter was shaken to his wooden core. He felt a swelling in his little wooden . . ." The fat man smirked briefly at the audience ". . . heart."

With all sorts of handclasps and hopeful gawkings, the puppet was laying siege to the blonde. She closed her eyes, smiled, shook her head, went on humming.

Carr noticed Jane picking her way through the tables. But she was moving away from him. He tried to catch her eye.

". . . and so Peter decided to follow the blonde home." The fat man made footsteps in an upper octave. *"Pink-pink-pink . . .* went his little wooden tootsies . . . *pink-pink-pink."*

Jane reached the platform and to Carr's astonishment, stepped up on it. Carr started forward, but the packed tables balked him.

Besides, contrary to his expectation, no one seemed inclined to bother Jane. Goldie was nowhere in sight, the noisy audience took no notice, and the fat man and the blonde apparently had decided to ignore her for the time being.

The blonde was making trotting motions with the puppet and the fat man was saying "Peter found that the blonde lived right next door to a furniture factory. Now Peter had no love of furniture factories because he'd once narrowly escaped becoming part of a Sheraton table leg. The screaming of the saws and the pounding of the hammers . . ." He did buzzy chromatic runs and anvil-chorusings ". . . *terrified* Peter. He felt that each nail was being driven right into his little wooden solar plexus, that the screaming saw was ruthlessly cutting off his precious wooden parts!"

Jane was standing near the blonde. Carr at last caught her eye. He thought he read there his own mixed feeling of pity and revulsion toward the noisy, mindless, beauty-blind horde.

He motioned her to come down, but she only smiled.

Slowly she undid the gilt buttons of her coat and let it drop to the floor.

"Finally, conquering his terror, Peter *raced* past the furniture factory and *darted* up the walk to the blonde's home . . . *pink-pink-pink-pink!*"

Jane had coolly begun to unbutton her white blouse.

Blushing, Carr tried to push forward, motioning urgently. She took no notice. He started to shout at her, but just then he realized something and the realization left him speechless.

The crowd wasn't reacting. It was chattering as noisily as ever.

They *were* blind. They *were* mindless. They couldn't contact anything that was outside of their mechanistic rhythm.

But that was ridiculous.

But that Jane should in reality be a strip-tease dancer at Goldie's Casablanca—that was ridiculous too. Or that she should be so drunk . . .

"Peter followed the blonde up the stairs . . . *trip-trip-trip* . . . and into her bedroom. He felt the sap running madly up his legs and into his little wooden . . . tummy."

Jane dropped her blouse, was in her slip and skirt.

Carr stood with his knee pushed forward against a table, swaying slightly, his hand still upraised like a drunken traffic cop ordering the world to stop.

"Then, his throat dry as sawdust with excitement, Peter *jumped* into bed with the blonde!" The fat hands tore up and down the keyboard. "And the blonde looked at Peter and said, 'Little wooden man, what now?'"

Jane looked at Carr and dropped the shoulder straps and let her slip fall away. Carr swallowed. Tears stung his eyes. Her breasts seemed far more beautiful than flesh ought to be.

And then there was, not a reaction on the part of the crowd, but the ghost of one.

Sudden silences at parties are a common experience. One moment everyone is talking. The next, all conversations halt at once. You look about foolishly. You vaguely think, according to your turn of mind, of the mathematics of coincidence, of an invisible spirit passing, or of some chemical or physical stimulus, such as a faint odor or an odd half-heard sound, affecting everyone, but too tenuous to register clearly on anyone's

97

consciousness. Then someone laughs and you're all talking again.

Such a momentary silence fell on Goldie's Casablanca. Even the fat man's glib phrases seemed to slacken and fade, like a phonograph record running down. His pudgy hands slowed, hung between cords. While the frozen gestures and expression of the people at the tables all hinted at words halted on the brink of utterance. And it seemed to Carr, as he stared at Jane, that heads and eyes turned toward the platform, but only sluggishly and with difficulty, as if all these people were dreaming and only half-wakened from their dreams, or as if, dead, they felt a faint, almost painful, ripple of life. They seemed to see and yet not to see Jane's naked breasts, to begin to forget at the same moment they become aware.

And although he knew it was ridiculous and that his mind was hazy with liquor, Carr felt that Jane was showing herself to him alone, and the stupefied audience were no more than cattle who turn to look toward a sound, experience some brief sluggish glow of consciousness, and go back to their cud-chewing and their dark wordless inner life.

Then, all at once, the crowd was jabbering again, the fat man was smirking and tittering, the blonde was fighting off a madly amorous puppet, and Jane was hurrying among the tables, her arms pressed to her sides to hold up her slip, with snatched-up coat and blouse trailing from one hand. As she approached, it seemed to Carr that everything else was melting into her, blurring off, becoming unimportant.

When she'd squeezed past the last table, he grabbed her hand. They didn't say anything. Their eyes took care of that. He helped her into her coat. As they hurried up the stairs and out the glass door, they heard the fat man's recitation die away like the chugging of a black greasy engine: "And what do you think little Alice found when she went up to the nursery?—her puppet Peter and her French doll Goldielocks in a most compromising position, oh, yes, a most . . ."

It was five blocks to Carr's room. The streets were empty. A stiff breeze from the lake had blown the smoke from the sky, and the stars glittered down into the trenches between the buildings. The darkness that clung to the brick walls and besieged the street lamps seemed to Carr to be compounded of excitement and terror and desire in a mixture beyond analysis. He and Jane hurried on, holding hands.

The hall was dark. He let himself in quietly and they tiptoed up the stairs. Inside his room, he pulled down the shades, switched on the light. A blurred Jane was standing by the door, taking off her coat. For a moment Carr was afraid that he might have drunk too much. He moved toward her quickly. Then she smiled and her image cleared and he knew he wasn't too drunk. He almost cried as he clapped his arms around her.

How strange it was. What she had been doing in Goldie's Casablanca was not exhibiting herself, but hiding; from *them*. Taking on protective coloration. To him alone, he was sure, had she been truly revealed. And it was this revelation that teased him, taunted him, now.

The coat and blouse were off. Suddenly and almost innocently the slip dropped, the last curtain between them. This was the true Jane, all of Jane. The Jane tempting, delectable, rosy between her big-nippled, big-aureoled, tiny breasts, ivory in the shaven area above her triangle of Venus. He tasted this throbbing curving flesh with his hands, then his seeking lips. As desire soared hotly within him, it mounted responsively in her. She gave herself to him completely, part by smooth part (so very smooth, indeed), and yet not solely giving, but taking. Drawing on him as he drew on her. First slowly, sensuously. Then at increasing pace, until theirs was the swift, searing throb of climatic love, waxing to a poignant ecstasy beyond anything either had ever known—and waning, waning, as the crested wave breaks and wanes, only to renew itself and again rise surgingly to a new peak of bliss.

After they had slept together he found himself realizing that he had never felt so delightfully sober in his life, though granting that the picture might change a bit if he made a sudden movement. From where he lay he could see Jane in the mirror. She'd thrown on his dressing gown and was mixing drinks for them. A faucet gurgled briefly. Then she came back and he turned over and hitched himself up on an elbow.

"Here," she said, handing him a glass.

He laughed. "I'm not sure what this will do to me. My mind's in a delicate state."

"Just a small one," she said. "To us."

"To us." They clinked glasses. Following her example, he drained his. She sat down on the bed and looked at him.

"Hello, darling," he said.

"Hello."

"Feeling okay?"

"Wonderful."

"Not worried about anything?"

"Of course not. What made you ask me that?"

"I don't know. You look sort of sad."

She smiled. "Isn't it all right for love to make you sad?"

"I suppose so, in a way."

"It makes you sad because when you've loved, you're empty and your guard's down. And you're a little frightened because right there before you is the one you love, so tender and easily hurt, and his guard's down, too."

"But then joy ought to follow the sadness, before it's even had a chance to get started." And he touched her arm, tugged gently at the dressing gown, but she just stayed smiling at him, and after a while he took his hand away.

"You're sure you're not bothered about anything?" he queried.

"Oh, darling," and it seemed to Carr that tears came into her eyes, making them bright, "this is the happiest night of my life. Whatever happens I want you to know that I love you utterly and completely."

He sat up a little. "Nothing's going to happen."

"Of course not. But I wanted you to know."

"Oh, sure." He hitched himself around a bit as to face her. "But now that you've brought up the question of what's going to happen to us, let's talk about—"

He faltered. It seemed to him that a black haze had suddenly raced across the room. He rubbed his eyes. When he took his hand away, the room was swimming.

"I didn't know I was that drunk," he muttered. "I never thought that just one more drink—"

He looked quickly at Jane. She hadn't moved. She still seemed to be smiling, very tenderly, almost pityingly. He turned his queerly heavy head toward the

100

little table by the bed. With an effort he brought the brown blur into focus. The surface of the table was bare.

"The powders!" he said, and he had difficulty forming the words. "You put them in my drink."

She didn't answer.

"Damn you,' he said, pushing himself toward her smudged image, "you've got to—"

He felt her hands on his shoulders, pushing him back.

"You'll be all right. You just need a little sleep." Her voice seemed to come from the floor above. He tried to fight her, but he couldn't lift his hands. The darkness was gaining fast.

"No I don't," he protested. "Ja . . . Plea . . ."

"Just a little rest."

"I won't forget you . . ." he croaked miserably, "I won' . . . I wo . . ."

She was leaning over him. For a moment his vision cleared and he saw her face streaming with tears, and her white neck, the unlossened dressing gown, and her breasts. Then the darkness narrowed in around her and closed like the iris diaphragm of a camera.

CHAPTER NINE

The Blank Hours

CARR MACKAY RUBBED his face against the pillow, rolled over, slitted his eyes open and grimaced at the bright narrow oblong of light beneath the shade.

He waited impatiently for the alarm clock to stop ringing. When the last tinkle finally came, his mind eagerly dove back inside his body and lost itself in countless vague awarenesses of weight and tension, little pleasurable aches.

Then, just as it seemed certain that he must drift off to sleep again, he briskly got up, stuck his feet in slippers, went to the window, pulled up the shade, looked at the street, sniffed rheumily at the air, and went to the bathroom.

A large washrag, drenched in water hot as he could get it, wrung out, and held to his chin and cheeks, elicited from him the morning's first smile. The lather felt good, too. He stroked it on thoughtfully, trying to get a uniformly thick coat, like a meringue pie.

When this job was completed to his satisfaction, he picked up his safety razor, squinted at it to make sure it was clean, screwed the handle until the blade had the proper tension, and looked at himself in the mirror. His nostrils twitched with friendly distaste.

"You're a dumb character, Carr Mackay," he said to himself in a kindly way, as he pulled the razor down his jaw. "Thirty nine . . . and an interviewer at an employment agency. That's the measure of your ability in the workaday world!" He finished the cheek with quick little chops, held the blade under the hot faucet, and started on the other cheek. The first stroke was always the most fun, like shoveling snow. "Oh, but your job's just a stepping stone? You're going places from there? In a month, you say, you'll be Mackay of Fisher and Mackay, editorial counselors? A little big shot?" Pulling his upper lip taut over his teeth, he tucked the razor under his nose and pulled it down carefully.

"Listen, Mackay, whom do you think you're fooling? Why not admit you're going to wriggle out of it at the first opportunity, even if you have promised Marcia? You know very well that you hate any and every new job, and that you doubly detest one in which you're supposed to dazzle other people. And even if you have to take it to placate Marcia, it's a foregone conclusion that you'll end up as Mr. Fisher's office boy. On top of all that, the thing's a pipe dream." Reversing the razor, he mowed his lower lip. "Oh, but something very different is going to come along, is it? Some totally unexpected event that will burst through the dull round of life and open up a world of mystery and delight? Mackay, my friend, we have been listening to that quaint notion of yours for a long time and we're getting very sick of it." He attacked his chin fiercely; it was the crab grass in the lawn of his beard.

"Put it this way: without exactly intending to, you've reached an equilibrium in life. Rather hard to work your way farther up, and you don't want to. And not too easy—ah! there's the fear!—to slide down." He started on his neck. Since he'd never quite decided which way the hair grew there, he shaved without confidence.

While reheating the washrag, he studied his shaved face. Odd, though he thought of Marcia, it didn't bring quite the same feeling of frustrated hunger as it usually did in the early morning. He felt this morning as if he were a neat little machine that could be trusted to go ticking along indefinitely without getting into any trouble—or much of anything else. Reassuring, but also depressing.

He buried his face in the steaming washrag.

Returning to the bedroom, he faced the question of whether to wear his blue or brown suit. A weighty decision—or were all those things decided for you in advance? He chose the brown. While slipping on the trousers, his glance fell on the empty surface of the table beside the bed. He felt a vague quirk of uneasiness. Should something be there? He decided not.

Standing in front of the dresser, he transferred to his pockets the objects neatly laid out on it, and brushed his hair with the military brushes. He glanced at Marcia's picture, curious as to its effect on him. She looked very cool and well-photographed. Strange, he thought, how we're tied to faces. He reminded himself that he and Marcia were due at the Pendleton's tomorrow night—Friday. That would give him another day and a half to brood about the Fisher business.

After a quick patting of his pockets to check whether he had everything he should, and a final glance around the room, he went out the door, locked it behind him, and trotted down the stairs. A glance at the blank-faced Carr in the mirror decided him that it was going to be a dull day.

On the street he bought a paper and swung aboard a bus that arrived on cue. He paid his fare and found a seat.

After the ride, he was faced with the morning's second important question. Reflex or free will, he ordered orange juice, an egg, toast, and coffee. While waiting for them, he continued with the paper—sports and comic page. Again he had a sense of things having been speeded up.

Half a block from General Employment he met Tom Elvested. They exchanged comments on the weather. Something was nagging at Carr's mind, though, as they

103

entered the office. There was a question he'd been meaning to ask Tom, but now he'd forgotten what it was.

Miss Zabel looked up from the rose she was posing in a slim-necked glass vase. She smiled at him. He smiled back. Then he noticed that the calendar pad on her desk said "Friday." He started to say something, then glanced surreptitiously at the dateline of his paper. He felt mildly astounded. It *was* Friday. And he'd been thinking it was Thursday—or had he? This damn job gave you softening of the brain—couldn't even remember the day of the week. Oh, well, so much better. Made it that nearer week-end. And he'd see Marcia tonight. Was his tux in shape? Of course.

He'd no sooner settled himself at his desk and got his things arranged than his first applicant appeared, and thereafter they came in a steady stream. Business was very brisk for a Friday. He had something to occupy him every minute.

In spite of that, after the first hour he began to get some more of those flashes of uneasiness that had troubled him in the bus. Little flickers of apprehension that came without warning and departed with a guilty swiftness, as if they had no right to be in his mind. For no good reason, certain things bothered him. The glass panel. The clock. A stubby end of pencil on his desk. Tom Elvested's back, which seemed so bulky. Miss Zabel's teetering walk.

He rather expected lunch with Tom and the gang to shake him out of his mood. But it almost made Carr ache to listen to Tom Elvested mouthing stale cracks about the coming election, between businesslike forksful of Hungarian goulash. He knew very well that Tom was an intelligent, discerning chap, but to listen to him now you'd swear he'd swallowed a phonograph record with a last month's news commentary on it.

Ernie and Acosta were as bad, and the fact that he himself felt more or less like a nervous robot was no consolation at all. The waitress seemed to be forever bringing their checks.

To top it, Tom had to lag behind with him on the way out and start talking about that intellectual girl-friend of Midge's and how they must have a date sometime together. It was all he could do to keep from being rude.

When he got back to the office his mood was worse than ever. He gritted his teeth. It was turning into one of those frightful days when every nod and smile takes an effort and you have to purse your lips or clench your fists under the desk in order to understand what people are saying.

One of those days when it's hard to keep track of what you're doing. He found he'd picked up the phone and dialed Marcia's number without any memory of the thoughts leading up to the action.

"Could we have dinner before the party tonight?" he asked her. "I'd like to talk to you."

"Sorry, but I can't make it. But if you call for me about eight, we might stop somewhere for a drink."

"Swell." He felt there was something he wanted to say to her, now, but he couldn't think what it was before she hung up.

Just then he heard the scrape of boots and saw a dumpy man in blue jeans approaching his desk—and felt patches of gooseflesh break out on his back.

Oh, he remembered the little man well enough from the day before yesterday. The trouble was that the figure stood out too vividly in his memory, like something in a nightmare.

He could remember with a feverish distinctness almost every word the man had spoken, the exact intonations, each gesture he had made.

He could picture precisely how the man smoked a cigarette.

But there were the most frightening gaps in his memory. He couldn't recall a word he himself had said to the man, or how he'd reacted to him, or how he'd handled the man's application. It was as if the dumpy man floated alone in space, a small blue god.

It was only with the greatest difficulty that he could recall his name—Jimmie Kozacs; and his occupation—magnetic inspector.

And now facing him across the desk, the man had the same quality of excessive reality as Carr's memory of him. As if he were sitting in the front row of a movie house and the little magnetic inspector, magnified many times, were towering over him on the screen.

Then, as if from a defective speaker at the back of such a movie house, he heard the man say, "Hello. I come about that Norcott job. It wasn't like they made it out to be."

Carr was conscious of asking him to sit down, of fumbling for his application blank and record card, of making some sort of conversation. He was conscious too, as the interview progressed, of Mr. Kozac's genially outraged complaints about what they expected a magnetic inspector to do out at Northcott.

But all the while he was hypnotized by Mr. Kozacs' excessive reality.

To look at that wholesome, reddish face with its upturned nose, and at the stocky, blue-jeaned body, and to be waiting, as it were, for them to get so solid that they'd break through the floor.

To rack your brain as to what conceivable connection there could be between such an innocuous face and the formless dread that kept surging through you until you almost wanted to retch.

And all the while to be talking to that face and scribbling memos for it, and finally to bid it goodbye and wish it better luck.

Just then Carr noticed a silly error in Mr. Kozac's application blank.

It was the date. It showed their first interview as having occurred on Tuesday, when of course it had been only the day before yesterday—Wednesday.

The dumpy man was just stepping past the next applicant approaching Carr's desk. Carr started to call him back and point out the discrepancy.

But before he could speak, his mind returned from the journey it had taken without waiting for his explicit bidding—a quick round-trip to last Sunday and back.

It brought numbing news.

Parts of Tuesday afternoon, Tuesday and Wednesday evenings, and all of Thursday, were blanks.

Maybe today isn't Friday. Maybe they're all wrong. Maybe half of Chicago has made a mistake.

No, Mackay! That's the way to shake your mind loose. That's the super-highway to the insane asylum. *You've got to face it.*

But what were you doing, then, during those blank spells? *What were you doing?*

Steady! That's a question that will have to be left unanswered for the present.

But what are you going to do now?

Go to a psychiatrist? Tell him about your "spells of amnesia"? Have him ask about your childhood, pull down the shade, shine lights in your eyes, work on your nerves—

No! You couldn't stand that and you know it. That would shake your mind loose for sure.

But there *is* something you can do. Something that'll at least keep the road open to sanity and safety. It isn't spectacular, though it'll take a sort of courage. You can simply keep doing what you're supposed to be doing. Go through all the motions of your daily routine without varying them an iota. There's safety in routine, Mackay. It keeps men going when nothing else will. You know, soldiers in battle, and all that. By following routine, you have the best chance of holding onto your mind.

You can start right now. Stand up—and did it ever occur to you, Mackay, that standing up is an interesting mechanical problem? Your bones are levers, your muscles are motors—you can feel the cables of sinew tighten smoothly. Smile—it gives you a crinkly feeling in your cheek, doesn't it? Shake hands with the next applicant. Note the moisture. Also the quality of the grip. Vigorous but jerky—that's a clue to character. Study his face— the smile, the gold fillings in his back teeth, the worried brown eyes yellow-flecked, the ripples of tension in the dusky skin around them, the alert nose, the eczema scars under the powder. That's a face for you, Mackay, a face to remember.

Rejoice, Mackay! Here's a new applicant—a whole new world for you to lose yourself in. I know it's hard, Mackay, but in an hour and thirty-seven minutes it'll be five o'clock. If you hold on until then and do what's expected of you, you can walk out of here with your mind intact and no one will have the faintest suspicion of what's happened to you. You'll be free, Mackay, free!

CHAPTER TEN

Time Out of Mind

CARR NUDGED HIS glass forward across the chromium surface.

The bartender reached for it. Carr turned toward Marcia. "Another?" he asked. "I'm one up on you."

She smiled but kept hold of the stem of her glass. The bartender flicked up Carr's and turned away.

"You want to have just the right amount of edge on you when you meet Keaton," she said. "He goes a lot by first impressions."

Carr nodded dutifully. Marcia looked very handsome tonight. Above the black dress her bare shoulders and neck were startlingly youthful. And on her face was that expression which Carr always found both exciting and disturbing—a look that incited daring, but threatened waspishness if the daring were not of just the right quality; a look that indicated she was intensely interested in you, but only in certain things about you.

Not, for instance, in your troubles. No matter how black.

"What's the matter, Carr? You're so silent."

"Nothing."

"One would almost think you weren't looking forward to meeting Keaton."

Carr finished his Manhattan. He touched his black tie. There was another uncomfortable silence. To break it, he started to talk at random.

"You remember Tom Elvested? He's been pestering me to go out with some mysterious girl he insists is just my type."

"Why don't you?" Marcia said quickly. "It might be very amusing."

Carr laughed. "I just mentioned it as an example of Tom's bull-headedness. Once he gets an idea—"

"But why not?" Marcia pressed. She might be young. That would be interesting for you."

"Nonsense," said Carr uncomfortably. "I gather she's a wet blanket. Some sort of timid intellectual. I mentioned it as an example . . ."

His voice trailed off. He looked at his empty glass. Marcia looked at him.

"Time we were going," she said.

In the taxicab she quickly turned and kissed him. Before he could respond she had moved away and was telling him the latest gossip of the publishing business. A few blocks and they were pulling up at the Pendleton's.

From the street, the brightly lighted windows of the huge third floor apartment looked like the amusement deck of a medium-size ocean liner ploughing through the night. There were even the strains of music echoing down.

There was a flurry of movement in the street. Another taxicab drew up behind theirs. A messenger boy with a cellophane box appeared from the opposite direction and ran up the walk. A large black dog, held on leash by a woman in furs, came snuffing toward Carr and he felt an abnormal twinge of fear. He and Marcia hurried up the walk. He held the door for her and for the couple which had emerged from the second taxi. The man thanked him with a slight bow. The girl, who had a delicately flushed British complexion, touched Marcia's hand and they chatted.

As Carr followed their nicely filled stockings up the gray-carpeted stairs, he tried to think of something to say to the other man. But instead he found himself wondering what would happen if he had another attack of amnesia. That possibility hadn't occurred strongly to him before, but now it obsessed his mind.

Was an amnesia attack like fainting, or like sleep? Would it hold off as long as you kept thinking about it? Presumably anything might set off. Really he must see a psychiatrist in spite of everything.

A shrill laugh of greeting came skirling down the stairs. He looked up and saw Katy Pendleton hanging over the landing like a fat doll with a face covered by tiny cracks. A fantastic green flower dripped from her hand.

"Look what Hugo sent," she cried to them. "He can't

come. Detained at the consulate." She waggled the orchid at Marcia and the British girl. "My dears, you look lovely. Come with me." She handed the cellophane box to the messenger boy. "No reply." Then quickly, to Carr and the other man, with a jolly grimace, "Mona will show you," and sweeping back through the door she revealed a sharp-faced Negro maid she'd been eclipsing.

As Carr stepped inside he saw that the Pendleton's apartment did have something of the layout of an ocean liner. Rooms opening to either side of two parallel central hallways. The big shadowy sun porch, its dark doors visible beyond dancing couples, might be the bridge. Next, the huge living room—main salon. Then a small stuffy-looking study hung with large, dark portraits—captain's cabin. Then a library—second salon. Finally the luxurious staterooms. Dining salon and galley presumably at the stern.

The West Indian stewardess—Negro maid, rather—showed Carr a bed heaped with coats and hats, to which he added his own. Returning into the hall he saw Marcia talking earnestly to a small man who wore a soft white shirt under his tuxedo. Carr stopped short, feeling an uncomfortable coldness mounting inside him.

The small man slumped, his arms a-dangle, his thin features slack with tiredness. But this appearance was deceptive. He had a tic. Whenever it convulsed the muscles of his cheek, his dark-circled eyes flashed a penetrating, critical glance, and his fingers curled. It was as if he lurked behind a curtain which small puffs of wind kept twitching aside.

Marcia raised eyebrows at Carr. Carr went resignedly, knowing this must be Keaton Fisher.

But the introduction was hardly over, the dark-circled eyes had only begun to quick-freeze Carr, the limp fingers had not quite finished a pulse-taking handshake—which the tic suddenly converted into a spasmodic grip—when Katy Pendleton, who had been pinning the green orchid to a half-protesting redhead, interrupted.

"Oh, Mr. Fisher, I've promised to introduce you to the Wenzels. You'll excuse us, I know."

Marcia touched Carr's arm. "Later." She hurried off.

Momentarily relieved, Carr found himself a cocktail and drifted into the library, where a number of lively discussions were going on.

Carr recognized several people. But he hesitated at deciding which group to join and the conversation went so fast that his clever remarks were constantly getting outdated. He felt rather like an awkward girl nerving herself for the right moment to start jumping rope.

His uneasiness was fast reaching a peak where he might blurt out any sort of remark just so as to be noticed, when Marcia came along and said she wanted to dance.

As soon as Carr had his arms around her, he realized that here was the only person he wanted to talk to.

His other impulses had been merest camouflage. Why in the world, when something fantastically strange and terrifying had happened to him, should he waste thought or time on this noisy herd? It suddenly struck him that of course he must tell Marcia about his mysterious amnesia attacks. Whatever had made him think otherwise? What was love if you didn't share? As they circled past the beaming brown faces of the musicians, he got set to tell her.

"Just as well Katy butted in," Marcia whispered softly and swiftly. "That wasn't the right time for your talk with Keaton. I've spoken to him and arranged things."

He nodded. "Marcia," he began with difficulty.

"Now listen carefully, Carr," she said. "In about ten minutes Keaton will drift away from the library and go into the study. I'll see to it that he's alone. You watch for him and make sure not to get tied up with anyone. A few moments later, drift along after him."

"All right," he said, "but first, Marcia, there's something—"

The music ended with a flourish. Marcia gave him a little push. "Now run along and watch Keaton," she said. "Oh, hello, Guy," and the next moment her back was turned and she was talking with a lanky, graying Mr. Pendleton.

Miserably, Carr returned to the library, picking up a cocktail on his way. The discussions were still going full tilt. Keaton Fisher was now dominating one of them, timing his points to his tic.

Carr shuffled from the edge of one group to another, smiling and nodding approvingly at some of the remarks, but apparently just enough to get himself accepted without really being noticed. Everyone seemed to have con-

111

cluded that he was just a vacuous sort of chap who
wanted to wander around nursing a drink. He was conscious of a growing wall between him and all the others.
A glass wall, perhaps, since it seemed to him that he
could no longer hear so well what was being said—there
was a humming in his ears.

Just then he noticed Keaton Fisher disappearing into
the hallway. As if by magic his anxiety vanished and
self-possession returned. Just as earlier he had been filled
with relief to get away from Keaton Fisher, now he felt
overjoyed at the prospect of getting back to him—anything, so long as it gave him something definite to do.

He veered for a moment toward the table of cocktails,
then checked himself and walked straight to the study,
pausing outside the door.

Keaton Fisher was inside and alone. He had picked
up a magazine and was studying the table of contents.
He was facing a little away from Carr. He was motionless
—except for the tic.

A childish play on words occurred to Carr. Keaton
Fisher had a tic. Therefore Keaton Fisher was ticking.
Like a clock.

Dark portraits of bearded men in last century's clothes
looked down on Keaton—amsked men like himself who
shrewdly eyed profits through the eyeholes in their faces.
Carr felt a rush of anxiety and apprehension.

Staring motionless at the same page of the magazine,
Keaton Fisher continued to tick.

Motionless—yet all at once he seemed to Carr to
double in height, to become a terrifying figure in which
was concentrated the quintessence of all the brasher
and more predatory qualities of the noisy world around
them—the world of out-thinking and out-smarting,
come-ons and killings, ads and headlines, slaps and
grabs, the world of the super-intelligent business-robots,
of the hyper-efficient modern machine-men.

Keaton Fisher went on ticking.

For the moment everything was wiped from Carr's
mind except the question of whether or not to enter this
room. He knew that he was faced with a decision that
would effect his whole future life. He knew that, as
happens much too often with such decisions, he was not
making it, it was being made for him by forces stronger
than any which consciousness could summon, but it was
being made nevertheless.

Keaton Fisher still ticked.

With a little gulping sigh that was almost a whimper of fear, Carr ducked back, darted to the cocktail table, drank one, picked up one, then another—he could pretend he was taking it to some woman—walked rapidly into the living room, edged along the wall past the dancers, opened the door to the dark sun porch, saw it was empty, sat down and began to drink in greedy little gulps.

When he put down the second glass beside his chair, reaction struck him a blow that made him writhe. He stared frantically at the dark windows with their reflected gleams of color from the dance floor. What he had done had shut him away from Marcia forever. This had been a last chance, a last test. It would be kidding himself to think differently.

He had scorned a splendid chance to make a real success in the world, a chance to push his head above the level of the nonentities, to clamber up to a level where you had some say about what happened to you.

He had doomed himself to lose his present job, to sneak away from his present environment, to go downhill for God knows how long, until the urges inside him gathered themselves for another try, if they still had the strength for that. Shame and vanity, he knew, would permit no other course.

But most of all, he had lost Marcia.

Perhaps it still wasn't too late. Perhaps—

He jumped up, hurried back to the living room, sidled past the dancers, entered the study.

It was empty.

He looked in the library. He saw Keaton Fisher talking with some other people. Marcia looked happy. Keaton Fisher also seemed in expansive spirits. As Carr watched, he laughed at something and patted Marcia's arm—just as his tic came.

Carr jerked back, hurried to the cocktail table, repeated his maneuver with the three drinks, and returned to the sun porch.

But now, as he drank in the darkness with the orchestra moaning behind him, there was a difference. Now that he had taken the irrevocable step, or been pushed into it, he hated everything about the surroundings in which the step had been taken. Those idiots! What right had they to create a society in which brash-

113

ness and machine-efficiency alone counted, in which the unambitious and fleshly-soft were tortured? Blind as bats to the truly important things of life. Jigging and hip-wagging like cogs and pistons while the world went God knows where. Sneering and jibing while time stole days from everyone and wouldn't give them back. Fighting for crumbs of prestige, while unknown dangers, like black sea monsters, silently circled mankind's vessel. For a moment Carr felt as if the Pendleton's apartment were truly a ship, with only one poor drunken fool crouched futilely on the dark and empty bridge. He braced himself against the crash of the rocks.

Then, as the liquor tightened its grasp, another feeling came: optimism, or rather its blustering and uncertain ghost. Why the hell should he think he'd lost Marcia? Didn't she love him? What difference did it make it she'd been trying to change his life and he wouldn't let her? That just showed he was strong. He'd get her and take her somewhere else and they'd have some drinks and he'd explain everything to her. Tell her about the amnesia for one thing.

He threw open the door to the living room and strode across the dance floor just as the orchestra was starting a new number. He stared at faces. He didn't care how rude he was. He just wanted to find Marcia.

Couples brushed him, but he did not move out of the way. What did he care for all these fools who so studiedly took no notice of him? For these pseudo-people who pretended not to notice a drunken man making a spectacle of himself! Smirking imbeciles! How he'd like to run amuck through them, knock down the men, rip the bright dresses off the women—especially those off-the-shoulder ones!

Then he saw Marcia.

She was on the other side of the dance floor, alone. He motioned urgently to her. Her eyes flashed past him with a smile.

She took some twirling steps, just by herself, as if to indicate how irresistible the music was. As she turned his way, he motioned again—an angry jerk of the forearm. But she ignored him.

Keaton Fisher danced past her with Katy Pendleton. Keaton called something to Marcia and she laughed.

She continued to twirl gracefully by herself—tauntingly, Carr felt. He grimaced at her and motioned a third time.

She smiled tantalizingly. Her arm seemed to rest on an imaginary shoulder, her back appeared to arch against an imaginary hand.

Carr thought she must be mocking him. It was as if she said, "This is fun. Don't you wish you were here in my arms? Wouldn't you give anything?"

And she kept it up, like an automation.

As if that thought had been a signal, all Carr's feelings of the evening, his anxieties over Keaton Fisher, his agonies over his decision, his reactions to the whole Pendleton world, crystalized in one frozen instant of drunken awareness.

It was as if all the life-fluid in the figures before him had drained away through a huge single gash.

Sober people feel, for brief moments, that all life and meaning have suddenly gone out of everything around them—the sounds, the words, the people. To a drunken person it is more intense.

It seemed to Carr, as he swayed there squinting, that the Pendleton's world wasn't real. These were window dummies dancing. The jabbering voices from the library were recordings, droning up from the hollow insides of animated statues. And look at the orchestra! See how the rigid brown hand thumped the base viol, while two other hands jerked up and down above the piano keys and yet another pair shifted along the saxophone. One saw such trios, made of painted tin, in the windows of toyshops. These were larger and of infinitely more skillful workmanship, but the music still came from somewhere else.

Glass walls, had he thought? These people were behind glass walls, all right, the glass panels of a showcase. They were toys grown to a size where their clockwork racket out-dinned the universe.

Even Marcia was just an elaborate mechanical doll. Somebody had stuck a key in her side, wound her up, and now she whirled and whirled.

Like Keaton Fisher, they were all just ticking.

In a moment they would realize his presence. Enraged that a living man had blundered into their mechanical saturnalia, they would rush at him, a metal tide, glittering, flashing, clashing, flailing him with their metal arms, stamping him with their metal feet. Even now—

115

He flinched, spun around, saw the door to the stairs, lunged for it.

Carr stared at the bronze lion as if it were the one object in an otherwise empty universe. Then stone, shadow and night soared into being, dwarfing the turmoil of feelings that had been spinning his mind and speeding his feet.

He looked around a little foolishly, realizing that he was standing in front of the Art Institute, on the lakeward side of Michigan Boulevard. He remembered the walk downtown only as a progression of things seen without being noticed. A distant electric sign beamed the time at him—3:39. He felt chill dribbles of sweat on his cheeks. His evening shirt was wet under the armpits. He put his hand to his throat, gathering up the lapels of his tuxedo.

He walked up the stone steps and touched the lion, gingerly, as a child might.

A little later he felt the impulse to walk. But not drivingly—just to drift.

As he moved north along the tremendous boulevard, an occasional whizzing car curtsied apologetically at the cross streets. He was still drunk enough to have an illusion of being very tall and moving majestically.

He veered across the boulevard and stood in front of the dark entry of the public library. Suddenly he realized that something was pulling him through the night, drawing him along by an indefinite number of strands fastened deep in his brain and heart—strands so gossamer thin that one could never possibly become aware of them unless some other force were to oppose them.

The pulls felt very real. It almost seemed to him that he could lean back against them, trusting to their force to keep him from falling.

And they lured. They carried a promise of mystery.

He concentrated with the fixity of a mystic, clearing his mind of all random thoughts and letting his sensation float free, trying to feel and respond to the pulls.

He yielded to them.

The streets were deserted and there was no wind. He passed a bare newsstand. His foot rustled a torn sheet of newspaper.

The pulls continued, though without strengthening. As if a magnet drawing him on were receding as he walked, keeping always the same distance.

116

Halfway down this block the pull abruptly changed direction, drawing him into a narrow alley, a mere slit between giant walls.

It was too dark to see. He held his hands outstretched and felt ahead with each foot before trusting his weight to the large cobblestones. He could guide himself in a general way by the vertical streak of smoky light shot with strange blue glows at the far end.

After perhaps twenty steps he halted uncertainly. He began to hear muffled laughter and talk, strains of raucous music.

As he edged along the dark alley, he wondered what it could be that he was following. Some actual trail in the pavement or air—chemical or electrical traces that impinged on the senses too subtly for conscious recognition? Or was it submerged memories of something that had happened to him before—perhaps during one of the amnesia attacks? Or even some kind of posthypnotic suggestion?

But thinking interfered with his ability to sense the trail. He must make his mind like that of an amoeba that automatically drifts towards the shadows.

He emerged at the other end of the alley.

He found himself looking into the window of a music store, scanning by streetlight the sheet music and record albums and toy instruments. For a while he stood with his face pressed to the glass door, trying to make out what was inside.

From nowhere, a title dropped into his mind. The Moonlight Sonata. His thoughts bent and shuddered as if from a gust of wind. For a moment he was about to remember everything . . .

He came to a movie theater. Green-eyed three-sheets leered at him from the lobby and clutched with white claws at shadowy female forms whose terror-stricken faces implored rescue. A sign in front said: *"You'll Stare! You'll Scream! You'll Shiver with Delicious Panic, as the Mad Monster Roams the Darkened Streets, Seeking His Prey!"*

In front of the box office, the oddest thing happened. The trail abruptly veered toward the curb and changed completely in quality. Up to this point it had been quiet, almost sedate, if you could use such words. Now it suddenly became wild, ecstatic, "hot"—the spoor of something crazy and joyful. Carr had come to a place where,

117

if he'd been a dog, he'd have given an excited yelp and bounded off into the brush.

He became suspicious. It wasn't only that the change in the trail frightened him with its suggestion of the abandonment of sanity.

Dogs usually bounded off at an angle because they'd struck a different scent.

There must be two trails.

He spent almost a quarter-hour beating back and forth. What made it so difficult was that every time he struck the "hot" trail, it ruined his ability to sense the other for several seconds. Eventually he managed to plot them out to his satisfaction.

The hot trail came from around the next corner, circled deliriously in front of the theater, then shot off across the street. The quiet trail made one of its side-tracks into the theater and then came out again.

He shook his head. It was all so utterly strange. As if the trails were two of his moods. One melancholy, almost soothing. The other mad, daredevil, crazily impudent.

After a couple of false starts he followed the quiet trail across the next street and down another block, where it turned a corner. It seemed to grow stronger, or perhaps that was because there was no longer a distinction.

He came into the business district. Here the feeling of hostile desolation, that had accompanied him for some time, increased markedly. It wasn't only that the liquor was dying in him. Back by the stores and theaters there had been at least the ghost of some sort of human excitement, however cheap and stale, the glamor of tawdry lures hung to enmesh human appetites. But these great looming office buildings, with their trappings of iron-work and facings of granite, actually wanted to be ugly. They gloried in their stony efficiency, their indifference to human desires, their gray ability to crush out happiness.

Carr's eyes went uneasily from side to side. Did that narrow black facade, shooting up dizzily, jerk forward a little, as if giving an inscrutable nod? There was something exceedingly horrible in the thought of miles of darkened offices, empty but for the endless desks, typewriters, filing cabinets, water coolers. What would a stranger from Mars deduce from them? Surely not human beings. Here

118

reigned grinding death, by day as well as night, only now it put off its disguises.

With a great roar a cavalcade of newspaper trucks careened across the next corner, plunging as frantically as if the fate of nations were at stake.

The feeling of active dread, that had first hit him on entering the business district, had increased. There was something that must not hear him, something that must not see him, something that under no circumstances must be allowed to know that it was heard or seen.

Easy enough to understand why a bunch of deserted skyscrapers should give a person a momentary shiver. But why should it give you that certainty of a gang bent on tracking you down? And why, in the name of sanity, should that feeling be tied up with such incongruous items as an advertisement for Wilson's Hams, a glass panel, a black dog on a leash?

And somehow the number three. Three things? Three persons? Three what?

His feeling of near-memory was mounting toward a climax. He was certain that each hollow in the stone treads had received his foot before; that each naked vista of steel-ribbed and sinewed shafts had trapped his wandering gaze.

It had grown quite light while he'd been thinking. The stars had all gone. He could even make out, some blocks distant, the giant statue of Ceres atop the Board of Trade building. He recalled that she had no face. Being too high for features to be discerned except from an airplane or by telescope, a blank curved surface of stone did just as well.

Then, close, in fact across the street, he noticed three figures. He leaned forward sharply, watching.

For a moment he thought they might be statues.

There were really four figures, but the fourth was that of a large black animal—doglike yet somehow feline.

The three taller figures seemed to be surveying the sleeping city, somberly, speculatively.

The first was standing beside the dog with one arm extended straight forward towards its neck, as if holding it on a short leash. The figure was that of a woman. There was the sheen of light, glistening hair, the flare of a wide-shouldered coat.

The second was a portly man.

The third was slenderer, taller, seemingly younger. His

119

head looked small and neat, though not bald. And as he extended his arm to point at something far off, his cuff seemed empty.

Flashes of memory flickered wildly in Carr's brain. He leaned forward a bit more and craned his neck, as if getting even an inch closer to the group might let him identify him.

It was still too dark for faces. Yet though he knew those three had faces and what the faces looked like, he found himself wondering if they, any more than the statue of Ceres, needed to wear faces now.

He leaned farther and farther forward.

He remembered everything.

CHAPTER ELEVEN

The Visible Woman

THE KNOB OF Carr's bedroom door kept turning around and back. First a slow, creaking rotation, until the latch bolt was disengaged. Then a push, so that the door strained against the inside bolt. Then the knob, suddenly released, would spin back with a rattle. Then it would start all over again.

From where he lay, fully clothed except for shoes and coat, Carr watched the knob, peering along his leg and through the intricate brass bars that rose at the foot of the bed. He breathed as shallowly as he could. Although his neck and shoulders ached, he kept his head in the same awkward jerked-up position it had assumed when he first heard someone at the door. All his faculties were concentrated on avoiding any betraying sounds.

An infinitesimal breeze stirred the drawn shade. A big fly buzzed lazily in the muted sunlight, hovered along the ceiling, dipped to the mantle, floated noisily across the room, hit the shade with a loud plop, fell to the sill, crawled along it for a while, buzzed, and then started hovering along the ceiling again.

Carr could hear the throaty breathing of whoever was

outside the door. Besides that sound there was a faint shuffling or scrabbling, as if a dog were trying to get in.

The doorknob kept on turning like a broken-down bit of machinery that refuses to gasp its last.

For a moment Carr thought the fly had lit on his forehead. It was just a trickle of sweat, but it was enough to make him jerk a little. The bedsprings creaked. His muscles tightened. His stiffened his aching, nearly trembling arms. The whole room seemed to become a wall-papered funnel narrowing down to the doorknob, which kept on turning and springing back just as before.

He could hear more than the breathing now. A querulous muttering as if whoever were outside was getting impatient.

The fly plopped against the shade, fell, and buzzed along the sill. A bit of laughter floated up from the street.

All the will power in the world could no longer have subdued the shaking in Carr's arms. Again the bedsprings creaked, so loudly that whoever was outside must surely hear.

Yet the rhythm of the knob did not change, though the mutterings grew a trifle louder. Carr strained his ears, but could not make out the words.

The shade swayed. The fly started on its trip across the ceiling. He shifted his weight from arms to buttocks, slid one foot to the floor. The springs creaked, but no worse than before. In a moment he was crouching beside the bed. The mutterings were still unintelligible. He took a cautious step toward the door.

The knob stopped moving. There was a scrape of metal on wood and the swish of water. Then footsteps plodding away from the door.

Carr hesitated. Then he quickly tiptoed to the door, eased open the bolt, paused again, opened the door a slit and peered out.

The cleaning woman was walking away, pail in one hand; mop, broom, duster, and dustpan in the other. Straggly plumes of hair stuck up from the rag wound around her hair. A damp, dirty blue apron was tied in a hard knot behind her waist. The heels of her shoes ran off at the sides.

Carr opened the door farther. He wet his lips. "Hello," he said huskily.

The cleaning woman kept walking away.

He stepped into the hall. "Hello," he called, getting control of his voice. Then, louder, "Hello!"

Not by a moment's hesitation, not by the slightest alteration in her trudging gait, did the cleaning woman indicate that she heard.

"Hello!" Carr shouted.

The cleaning woman disappeared at an even pace down the stairs. Carr gazed after her. But his mind was listening to the drone of long-forgotten phrases from a college psychology class:

> To explain human behavior, it need not be assumed that consciousness exists. After all, we can never penetrate to the inner life of other individuals. We can never prove that such an inner life exists. But we need not. All the actions of human beings can be adequately accounted for on the assumption that human beings are unconscious mechanisms.

He edged blindly back into his room, bolted the door behind him, slumped against it.

At least, he told himself, the things at his door had not been what he had most feared.

But it had been almost worse.

Why, he asked himself, had he bothered to shout? Why had he sought last, unnecessary confirmation?

He already knew, had known ever since he had recovered his memory and fled from the streets.

Knew what he had known, known and rejected, at least four times before: when he had been ignored by the dumpy man and the doctor at General Employment, when he had watched Marcia in her bedroom, when he had spied on Jane's parents in their apartment, when he had run away from the Pendleton party.

But then he had known it only for fleeting moments.

This time it had gripped his mind for hours.

It was insane, incredible.

But it was true.

Nothing else could explain his experiences.

Jane knew, the small dark man knew, those other three knew.

And now he knew.

The universe was a machine. The people in it, save for a very few, were mindless mechanisms, clockwork things of flesh and bone. So long as you made the proper clock-

122

work motions, they seemed to react intelligently. But when you stopped, they went on just the same. When you quit being part of the clockworks, they ignored you.

How else explain the times when he had been ignored? By the dumpy man, Tom and the doctor. By the desk clerk at Marcia's and by Marcia herself, when he had come minutes ahead of the clockwork rhythm. By Jane's parents. By Marcia at the Pendleton party—she hadn't been pretending to dance with someone as she twirled by herself; she had been mindlessly dancing with another clockworks figure (himself) that had moved from its proper place in the clockworks.

How else explain the times when he and Jane had been ignored? In the tavern, in the music shop, at the movie house, at the chess club. In the stacks of the library, in the streets of the Loop, at Goldie's Casablanca. Or when Fred and he had been ignored—that crazy ride that should have set people staring and a dozen police cars and motor-cycles on their trail; and that crazy, unnoticed pursuit through the library.

How else explain the times when *those other three* had been ignored? The slap. Miss Hackman going through his desk. Mr. Wilson helping himself to the cigarettes. Their open talk in the tobacco shop and in front of Jane's parents.

How else the things that *hadn't fitted?* The dumpy man talking to the air. Pianos that played themselves and elevators that rose without occupants. Marcia calling him about the "wonderful evening" they'd spent together, when actually he'd run away. (For a moment he had a ghostly glimpse of her talking to an invisible companion at the Kungsholm, the waiter setting loaded plates before an empty chair. Jane's mother stroking non-existent hair, whimpering to an absent girl. And now the cleaning woman mindlessly trying a door that, in the vast operation plan of a clockworks universe, was not supposed to be bolted; repeating the action, like a toy obstructed in mid-performance, until the appointed time came for her to finish cleaning his room and go away.

There *were* no other explanations. The universe *was* a machine. Teeming Chicago was a city of the dead, the mindless, the inanimate, in which you were more alone than in the most desolate wilderness. The face you looked at, the faces that looked at you, that smiled and

123

frowned and spoke, had behind them only black emptiness.

Except for a few, a mostly horrible few.

What might some people do if they awakened to the knowledge that they alone had minds and consciousness, that they could do what they wanted and the machine could not stop them, that all authority was truly blind?

They would run amuck like soldiers in a conquered city, like drunken thieves in a department store at night. Treating all the people around them like the lay-figures they were. Exulting in their power. (He saw in his mind those three looking down at a sleeping Chicago.) Obeying all their hidden impulses. Satisfying all their secretest, darkest desires.

A few of them might band together, perhaps because they had awakened together. Say a wall-eyed blonde and an affable-seeming older man and a young man without a hand . . .

And a beast.

Jane had written, "Some animals are alive." And he, Carr, had once been noticed when he shouldn't have been, by a cat.

Yes, a few might band together. But except for that, they would be intensely suspicious. Afraid that some greedy, merciless group like themselves might become aware of them and destroy them, because absolute tyrants always fear and hate each other. Afraid, above all, that other people might come alive, more and more people, and punish them for their crimes.

As they satisfied their desires, as they had their "fun," they would guiltily watch for the slightest signs of true life around them, in order to crush it out.

That was why those three had trailed Jane, why they had wanted to "check" on her.

The slap had been a test. If Jane had reacted to it, she would have been lost.

That was why Miss Hackman had searched his desk—for signs that he was something more than a mindless automaton.

That was why the small dark man with glasses was afraid. That was the great danger against which Jane had warned him, the "private underworld" she didn't want to drag him into.

Three people preying on the dead city of Chicago,

watching for the faintest hints of consciousness in the lay-figures around them.

Carr realized that he was shaking. Mustn't they have seen him staring out the window at them this morning, conspicuous against the otherwise drearily unbroken facade? Mightn't they have followed him here from the Caissa Chess Club? Mightn't they even now be coming up the stairs, or standing noiselessly outside the door at which he was staring so fearfully?

He clenched his hands. All this was insanity, he told himself, a paranoid's nightmare.

But . . .

His throat ached. He went to the bathroom, drank a large glass of water, set it down on the stained bowl. Then he lay down again on the rumpled bed. Fatigue smarted behind his eyelids, was like a fever in his flesh.

Presently he fell asleep.

When he awoke it was dusk. The room was all soft shadows. The window shade seemed faintly phosphorescent. His face felt fresh, as if it had just been sponged.

Instantly his thoughts began to race again, but the cooling refreshment of sleep had given them an entirely new perspective.

He had teetered on the edge of insanity, he told himself.

He had fallen victim to a terrible delusion.

He must root it out of his mind as quickly as possible.

He must talk to someone, someone who was close to him and sensible, and convince himself that it was a delusion.

Marcia—

She was real. She represented the businesslike normal side of things.

She'd be home now.

Of course he'd insulted her pretty badly the last time he'd been with her, leaving her that way at the Pendletons'.

Still, she was fair. She'd listen. She'd understand. She'd relieve his haunting anxiety.

He got up and rapidly put on his shoes and coat. He tried not to let his thoughts or emotions wander. His purpose was to get to Marcia before he lost the feeling of confidence with which he had awakened—the saving conviction that all his hideous delusions had been nightmarish fancies.

He met no one on the stairs except his slinking counterpart in the mirror. The entrance hall below was also empty, and dark. Then he pulled open the door and stepped out into what he assured himself was not a city of automatons.

A man was passing by at the foot of the steps, a little old man in a brown coat and hat, with deep-set eyes that scowled ahead and lips that worked as if he were muttering to himself.

Carr had the impulse to call out to him, to engage him in conversation, to assure himself at once of the falsity of his delusion.

But strangers sometimes ignored you when you spoke. Especially crazy-looking ones.

No, it must be someone closer, someone who couldn't ignore him.

Marcia—

He walked rapidly. The sky was almost dark and a few stars could be seen. Soft glows from apartment windows made grotesque shadows. At intervals, streetlights glared. Narrow passageways between buildings were vertical black slits, except where side windows spilled illumination over brick walls a few feet away. Little shrubs crouched back against basement walls.

It was quiet. There were few figures on the streets. He tried unsuccessfully to avoid looking at the eyes of those he passed.

But people were that way in the city, he reminded himself. They'd pass you a foot away and not by the faintest flicker of their gaze betray an awareness of your existence.

This was Chicago, he told himself. Over three million inhabitants. A bustling metropolis.

Only tonight it was very quiet.

He had only one more street to cross before he came to Marcia's apartment—that corner just ahead where there was a small cluster of lighted signs. On this side, a restaurant and a cleaner's, the latter closed, both in an apartment hotel. On the other side, across the street, to his right, a cocktail bar decorated by scalloped banks of small electric lights.

He wasn't fifty feet from the corner—in fact he had almost entered the pool of light under the last street lamp —when he saw Marcia. She was wearing a dark dress

126

with a white flower pattern. She was carrying a square black handbag. She turned north toward her apartment.

Carr stood still. There was the person he most wanted to see, but now that he'd found her, he hesitated. Just as with the little old man passing the apartment steps, something held him back from making the move, from speaking the word that would relieve him.

He watched Marcia cross the street, walk into the pool of light on the other side, walk out of it.

He still hesitated. He felt a growing agitation. He looked around indecisively.

His glance took in a figure standing across the street, its slim, college boy form and cropped hair silhouetted by the bright glow of the scalloped lights, its face in shadow.

There was something familiar about the man. Carr automatically stared at him, trying to recall where he'd seen him before.

The man glanced behind him as if to reassure himself that Carr wasn't looking at someone else. Then he turned back. There was a tiny flash of white from the lower part of his shadowed face, as if he had shown his teeth in a smile. He waved to Carr jauntily.

As he did so, Carr realized that he *did* want to be with Marcia, walking at her side, in his proper place, accounted for, not alone in this dreadfully empty city.

For only a bit of hooked metal came out of the up-raised cuff across the street.

Everything stood out sharply as an engraving to Carr. He knew without counting that there were sixteen bulbs in each of the scallops, that inside the bar were walls stenciled with nymphs and satyrs, three nymphs and two satyrs to each panel, that the wide sidewalk in front of the bar was divided crosswise into blocks of three.

The handless man started toward him, entreating him to wait with another jaunty wave.

Carr pretended not to see. He turned north. Marcia was a small silhouette a quarter of a block away. He started after her at as brisk a pace as might still seem natural.

"Hold on a moment, would you?" The handless man called after him. The voice was rather high, but cool and pleasant, with an Eastern accent.

He knew he must not answer. Once give them proof that he was alive—

He pretended not to hear. He gained the opposite curb,

thankful that an approaching car had allowed him to lope for a few steps.

"Stop a minute, please," the handless man called. "There's something I want to tell you."

Carr's gaze clung to Marcia's flowered dress. Thank God, she was walking slowly. He went through a little pantomime of recognizing her, to justify a further increase in his pace.

"Please stop," the handless man called. "I'm sure I know you."

It was a dark stretch. The apartment Carr was passing boasted a hedge. Parked cars, gleamingly washed but filled with gloom, made another wall.

The footsteps behind him were gaining. Marcia was still some distance off. Carr fought to keep from running.

"You're not very polite," the handless man called. "After all, I'm a cripple, though it doesn't slow me down."

The footsteps were very close now. Although Marcia was hardly twenty feet away, it seemed to Carr that there might as well be a trench deep as the world between him and her.

The footsteps were just behind him. A toecap flicked the lower edge of his field of vision. A voice said in his ear, "Do stop now," and he felt his shoulder brushed by something like a talon.

Carr darted forward a few steps, slid his arm around Marcia's and said in as gay a voice as he could manage, "Hello, dear!"

Marcia did not turn her head. Not by the slightest break in her stride did she betray that she was aware of his existence. Even her arm, under his hand, was like a stick of wood.

The other footsteps dropped back a little.

"Please don't cut me," Carr whispered urgently. "I know how you feel about the way I behaved last night, but I can explain."

She turned, pulling away from him. He realized they had reached her apartment hotel.

The footsteps behind them speeded up.

Carr followed her up the walk. "I must come in with you."

Still she did not recognize his presence. She jerked at the door before he could reach it. He ducked through after her.

128

They crossed the lobby together. The clerk was leaning on the counter, chin in hand, so that his gold seal ring gleamed and his coat sleeve fell back, exposing the gold cuff link.

His eyes ogled them. He opened his mouth—there was the flash of a gold filling—and said, elaborately, "Good evening, Miss Lorish."

"Good evening," said Marcia, curtly.

Carr heard the door open and close behind them. Then the footsteps, crisp on the tiling, soft on the carpeting, swiftly over-taking them.

The elevator was waiting. Marcia stepped in and jabbed quickly at the seven button. Carr barely slipped through as the door started to close. Swiftly turning, he saw a hook blotted out by the closing door. The cage started up.

Carr felt a surge of partial relief, but then instantly the bigger fear closed in.

Marcia *was* ignoring him so utterly. She hadn't given him a single sign. As if, behind that beautiful impatient face, there were nothing, absolutely nothing . . .

No, that couldn't be true, he told himself. Mustn't be—not with her so close and the two of them locked in this little cage.

And as for Marcia, she was just being cruel. There'd been times before when she'd ignored him as a punishment.

"Darling," he began.

The cage stopped. Marcia jerked at the door and darted out. Carr hurried after her down the hall.

Marcia had her key out and the door to her apartment open in a single movement. The latter was almost slammed in Carr's face.

She must be aware of him, or she wouldn't be acting this way, he tried to assure himself as he pushed in after her. Her quick, angry movements pointed at her realization of his presence.

"Marcia, please stop acting so childish," he managed to say.

She tossed her handbag in a chair, hurried into the kitchen. He started after her, hesitated, moved around nervously.

She came out of the kitchen. She had a highball in her hand.

She set the drink down on the small table at his elbow, and went on into the bedroom.

Carr could hardly realize it for a moment, his relief was so great.

She was aware of him. By that simple action she'd admitted his presence.

All the rest of her behavior had been just temperament, her peculiar captiousness.

He picked up the drink and took a grateful gulp.

But as he did so, he noticed a piece of notepaper near it, covered with Marcia's handwriting.

His own name was at the top.

Transferring the drink to his other hand, he picked it up.

Dear Carr:

I recognized the power in you, Carr, the fiery cleverness, the talent for the grand gesture. But you would not use them. You could have been a prince. But you chose to be a hireling. Many times I guided you into situations where you would have the opportunity to find your real self. Again and again I got only the equivalent of a slap in the face for my pains. I was patient. I knew you'd been in a rut for a long time and I made allowances. But this last incident was too much for me. When you coldly turned down Keaton Fisher's magnificent offer—the offer of a man who has got to the top with no more ability than you, without your looks, and in spite of a lot more hindrances than you've had to cope with—when I watched you rudely reject that man's generous offer, I knew it was the end of things between you and me.

Here's a word of advice, if in the future you should ever decide that you're tired of being a hireling and would like to attempt the bigger role. If you want a woman to think you a prince, you must act like a prince in all ways. If you want to be with big people, you must be a big person. If you want life exciting and dangerous, you must be the size of danger and excitement.

But don't try to use that advice to win me back, for it can't be done. Save it for some other girl. Keaton Fisher isn't handsome, but he knows how to use what he has and he isn't afraid of taking risks.

And now, dear, the best of luck

Marcia

When supernatural terror prefaces an emotional wound, the latter is deadened. Still, as the letter dropped from Carr's hand and he heard Marcia coming from the bedroom, he felt a stab of mingled jealousy and self-pity hard to endure.

Her hand brushed the table beside him, she hesitated a moment, then stood in the center of the room.

Now that she knew he knew, he told himself, she must be waiting for him to go, perhaps preparing herself to reject some final appeal, setting her expression in obdurate lines.

But instead she was smiling. Smiling in a particularly unpleasant, animal-like way.

And gesturing in a peculiar fashion with her right hand.

And still not looking at him.

Carr felt a mounting horror as he watched her.

He tried to tell himself that he didn't understand what her gestures meant.

Tried to tell himself that they weren't the movements of someone sipping from a highball glass that wasn't there.

Tried to tell himself that when her hand had brushed the table, it hadn't been to take up the drink she had left there.

Because that would mean she hadn't made the drink for him, but for herself; that she hadn't recognized his presence; that the terrible delusion that had tortured him back at his room was true.

And that *mustn't* be.

"Marcia!" he called sharply.

She licked her lips.

Mustn't, he repeated to himself. Nothing could write you a letter to hurt you so and yet be a mindless machine.

He moved toward her. "Marcia!" he cried desperately and took her by the shoulders.

Then, under his hands, the moment he touched her, he could feel her muscles go rigid. She began to shake. Not to tremble, but to shake, to vibrate like a piece of machinery that's about to tear itself apart. He jerked away from her.

Her face was flushed, her features screwed up like a baby's.

From her lips came a mumbling that grew louder. It was, Carr realized with a gust of horror, exactly like the chattering of the dumpy man.

Or rather, the image sprang into Carr's mind as he broke away toward the door, like the meaningless noise of a phonograph record running backwards.

CHAPTER TWELVE

Bleached Prostitute

CARR GAZED UP at huge, grainy photographic enlargements of women in brassieres and pants painted bright orange. A sign screamed, "Girls and More Girls!"

Around him, lone dreary figures of men slouched purposelessly.

He realized that he was on South State Street, and that he had been searching for Jane Gregg through the nightmares of Chicago and his own mind ever since he had fled stealthily from Marcia's apartment some hours ago.

Jane was the only person in the world for him now. The only person who would answer when he spoke. The only person behind whose forehead there was an inner light.

Except for a few others best not thought of.

He had gone to every place he and Jane had been, fruitlessly. Now he had come to one place he remembered her speaking of.

Around him the signs glared, the dance music groaned, the automatons slouched through the dirty shadows. Chicago, city of death, mindless metropolis, peopled by millions of machines of flesh and bone that walked and worked and uttered phonograph words and rusted and went to the scrap heap.

Dead city in a dead universe. Dead city through which he was doomed to search forever, futilely.

He was glad that the nightmares inside his mind had helped to shut it out.

For a fleeting moment he had a vision of Marcia's face as he had last seen it. He expected the stuff behind the forehead of the vision to ooze from the eyes in black tears.

He passed a slot-like store that said TATTOOING, then a jumbled window with three dingy gilt balls overhead. In front of it lounged two figures of men in dark

132

slickers. They somehow stood out from the other dreary automatons.

As he crossed the street, a taxicab drew up ahead of him at a dull-windowed drugstore. The fat figure of the driver squeezed out and hurried inside. As Carr passed the drugstore, he noticed him dialing at an open phone. A line of dirty collar was creased between greasy-coated bulky shoulders and thick red neck. He heard the motor softly chugging.

Ahead lights thinned, sidewalks became emptier, as South State approached the black veil of the railway yards. He passed the figure of a woman. The face was shadowed by an awning, but he could see the shoulder-length hair, the glossy black dress tight over the hips and thighs, and the long bare legs.

He passed a sign that read: IDENTIFICATION PHOTOS AT ALL HOURS. He passed a black-windowed bar that said: CONTINUOUS ENTERTAINMENT.

He thought: I will search for Jane forever and never find her. I will search for Jane . . .

Carr stopped.

. . . I will search for Jane . . .

Carr turned around.

No, it couldn't be, he thought. This one's hair is blonde, and the hips swing commonly in the tight black dress.

But if he disregarded those two things . . .

The hair had been unevenly blonde. It could be, undoubtedly was, bleached.

The walk could be assumed.

He was beginning to think it *was* Jane.

Just then his glance flickered beyond the shoulder-brushing blonde hair.

A long black convertible drew up to the curb just this side of the taxi, parking the wrong way. Out of it stepped the handless man.

On the other side of the street, just opposite the girl in black, stood Miss Hackman. She was wearing a green sports suit and hat. She glanced quickly both ways, then started across.

Halfway between Carr and the girl in black, Mr. Wilson stepped out of a dark doorway.

Carr felt as if his heart were being squeezed. This was the finish, he thought. The end of Jane's long, terrified flight. The kill.

Unless . . .

The three pursuers closed in slowly, confidently. The girl in black didn't turn or stop, but she seemed to slow down just a trifle.

Unless something happened to convince them that he and Jane were automatons like the rest. Unless he and Jane could put on an act that would deceive them.

It could be done. They'd always been doubtful about Jane.

But she couldn't do it alone. She couldn't put on an act by herself. But with him . . .

The three figures continued to close in. Miss Hackman was smiling.

Carr wet his lips and whistled twice, with an appreciative chromatic descent at the end of each blast.

The girl in black stopped.

Carr slouched toward her swiftly.

The girl in black turned around. He saw Jane's white face, framed by that ridiculous blonde hair.

"Hello, kid," he called saluting her with a wave of his fingers.

"Hello," she replied. Her heavily lipsticked mouth smiled. She still swayed a little as she waited for him.

Passing Mr. Wilson, Carr reached her a moment before the others did. He did not look at them, but he could sense them closing in behind him and Jane, forming a dark semicircle.

"Doing anything tonight?" he asked Jane.

Her chin described a little movement, not quite a nod. She studied him up and down. "Maybe."

"They're faking!" Miss Hackman's whisper was very faint. It seemed to detach itself from her lips and glide toward his ear like an insect.

"I don't think so," he heard Mr. Wilson whisper in reply. "Looks like an ordinary pickup to me."

Cold prickles rose on Carr's scalp.

"How about us doing it together?" he asked Jane, pretending there was no whispers, no people behind them, forcing himself to go on playing the part he had chosen.

She seemed to complete a calculation. "Sure," she said, looking up at him with a suddenly unambiguous smile.

"Pickup!" Miss Hackman's whisper was faint as before, and as contemptuous. "I never saw anything so amateurish. It's like a highschool play."

Carr slid his arm around Jane's, took her hand. He

134

started with her down the street, toward the brighter lights. He heard the footsteps of the three keeping pace.

"But it's obviously the girl!" Miss Hackman's whisper was a trifle louder. "She's just bleached her hair and trying to pass as a whore."

As if she feared Carr might turn, Jane's hand tightened spasmodically on his.

"You can't be sure," whispered Mr. Wilson. "Lots of people look alike. We've been fooled before. What do you say, Dris?"

"It's the man all right," the whispered voice of the handless man responded. "But I followed him for a while tonight and I think he's okay."

"But if it's the same man. . . ?" Miss Hackman objected. "Remember I saw him with the girl at the employment office."

"Yes," Mr. Wilson responded, "and we decided that she'd tricked us there and he wasn't a real accomplice at all. Which should indicate that this can't be the girl."

Carr felt the whispers falling about them like the folds of a spiderweb. He said loudly to Jane, "You look swell, kid."

"You don't look so bad yourself," she replied.

Carr shifted his arm around her waist, brushing her hips as he did. But his eyes were searching the street ahead. The scene had not changed. The machinery of Nickel Heaven was in full blast. The two men in dark slickers across the street had been joined by two more. The taxi in front of the drugstore was still chugging. Fringing the field of his vision to either side, were blurred bobbing segments of Mr. Wilson's panama hat and pinstriped paunch and Miss Hackman's green garbardine shirt and nyloned legs.

"You agree with me about the girl, don't you, Dris?" Mr. Wilson asked.

"I think so." But this time the handless man's voice lacked assurance. "But I can't be sure, because . . . well I'm not absolutely sure about the man. It's just possible that he fooled me."

Miss Hackman leaped at the opportunity. "Exactly. And I think they're still faking. Let me test them."

Through the skimpy dress Carr felt Jane shaking.

"Put that away!" Mr. Wilson whispered sharply.

"I will not," Miss Hackman replied.

They were almost at the corner. They were passing the

black convertible. The figure of a bleary-eyed man in a faded blue shirt lurched up onto the curb and came weaving across the sidewalk. Carr steered Jane out of his way.

"Disgusting," Jane said.

"I'd have taken a crack at him if he'd bumped you."

"Oh, he's drunk," Jane said.

"I'd have taken a crack at him anyway," Carr asserted, but he was no longer looking at her. The cab driver had come hurrying out of the drugstore.

"Come on, kid," said Carr suddenly, stepping ahead and pulling Jane after him. "Here's where we start to travel fast."

"Oh, swell," breathed Jane. Her eyes went wide as she looked at the taxi. They hurried toward it.

Beyond the corner, the men in dark slickers felt the pawnshop window and headed toward them.

Miss Hackman's whisper was almost a wail. "They're getting away. You've got to let me test them."

The cab driver ducked his head to get in. Simultaneously Carr reached for the door.

"It might be better . . ." came Dris's voice.

Cold as ice, Carr held the door for Jane. From the corner of his eye he saw Miss Hackman's hand. In it was one of the stiff daggerlike pins from her hat.

"Well . . ." began Mr. Wilson. Then, in an altogether different voice, still whispered, but tense with agitation and surprise, "No! Look! Quick, we've got to get out of here!"

Carr stepped in after Jane, slammed the door, dropped into the seat. The taxi jerked forward, but behind them he heard a more powerful motor roar into life.

He ventured a quick look back.

The black convertible was speeding down South State, away from them.

At the curb they had left stood a knot of men in dark slickers.

Carr unlocked the door to his room, hurried to the windows, pulled down the shades, went back to the door, looked down the dark hall, listened for a few moments, finally locked and bolted the door.

Only then did he switch on the light.

"Do you really think it's safe here?" Jane asked him. Framed by the amateurishly bleached hair, her face looked small and tomboyish.

"Safer than taking our chances somewhere else," he told her. "I don't think they know my address yet." He frowned. "What do you suppose scared them off at the end?"

"I didn't know they were scared of anything," she said.

"There were those men in slickers . . ." He began doubtfully.

"They aren't scared of men," she told him, her gaze straying toward the bolted door.

"I'll get us a drink," he said.

As he added water to whisky in the bathroom he remembered the motionless head and fat neck of the thing driving the taxi as they had slipped out at a red light near La Salle and Grand. Everything around him grew distorted-looking and horribly solid. It seemed to him impossible, in a universe of recalcitrant mechanisms, that he should be able to unscrew the cap of a whisky bottle, to turn a faucet, even to push aside the thick air as, the dingy white floor seeming to rock under his feet, he dizzily fought his way out into the bedroom.

Jane sprang toward him.

"It's all impossible," he assured her gaspingly. "We're both insane."

She grabbed his arm above the elbow, squeezed it. "I've said that to Fred," she told him unpityingly, "many times. And to myself."

He squeezed his eyelids. The floor steadied under him. She took one of the drinks from him. He drank a mouthful from the other.

"An insane delusion could be shared . . ." he began.

She just looked at him.

"But if we aren't insane," he continued tormentedly, "what's made the world this way? Have machines infected men, turning them into things like themselves? Or has man's belief in a completely materialistic universe made it just that? Or . . ." He hesitated ". . . has the world always been this way—just a meaningless mechanical toy?"

She shrugged.

"But why should *we* be the ones to awaken?" he went on with growing agitation. "Why, of all the billions, should we two be the ones to grow minds, to become aware?"

"I don't know," she said.

"If we only knew *how* it happened to us, we might have some idea . . ." He looked at her. "Jane," he said, "how did it happen to you? When did you first find out."

137

"That's a long story . . ."

"Tell it to me"

". . . and I'm not sure it explains anything."

"Never mind, Jane. Tell it to me."

She looked at him thoughtfully. "Very well," she said softly. She sat down on the edge of the bed, almost formally, and took a sip of her drink.

"You must think of my childhood," she began, "as an empty, overprotected, middle-class upbringing in a city apartment. You must think of me as unhappy and frightened and lonely, with a few girl friends whom I thought silly and ignorant and at the same time more knowing than myself.

"And then my parents—familiar creatures I was terribly tied to but with whom I had no real contact. They seemed to go unhappily through a daily routine as sterile as death. They got excited over newspaper stories that didn't have anything to do with them. And yet they were blind to a thousand strange and amazing things that were happening right around them.

"The whole world was a mystery to me, and a rather ugly one. I didn't know what people were after, why they did the things they did, what secret rules they were obeying. I didn't know that there were neither rules nor purposes, only mechanical motions. I used to take long walks alone, trying to figure it out, down by the river, or in the park." She paused. "It was in the park that I met the small dark man with glasses."

Carr looked up. "What's happened to him now?" he asked nervously.

She shrugged. "I haven't any idea. The last time I saw him was when you came to the library."

"You say you first met him in the park?"

"I didn't exactly meet him" she replied. "I just noticed him watching me. Usually from a distance—from another path in the park, or across the lagoon, or through a crowd of people. He'd watch me and follow me for a way and then drift out of sight and maybe turn up farther on." She hesitated. "I had no idea, of course that he was already outside the machine—I mean Life—and attracted to me because I could sometimes see him and so must be half awakened to consciousness. But suspicious and afraid of me too and wanting to make sure of me first.

"I sometimes thought he was something I'd made up in my mind. He had the oddest way of fading into the shrub-

138

bery, of slipping behind people, of disappearing when there seemed to be no place to diappear to. He reminded me of my cat Gigolo in one of his prowling moods, when one moment he'd be lying on the cushion looking at me, and the next peeking in from the hall—and no memory at all in my mind of his moving from one place to the other. Yes, it was like that. I had the feeling that I could blink the small dark man on and off, if you can understand that. I know now that was because I was sometimes almost fully awake to consciousness—when I'd see him—and then almost asleep again. I'd see him and intend to remember him but somehow I wouldn't think of him again until he popped up the next day.

"That was the inertia of the machine asserting itself. Because the machine—the big machine called Life—always wants you to live according to the preordained pattern, even if you do grow a mind; in a sort of trance, as it were. That's why it's so easy to forget what you experience outside the pattern, why a simple drug like the chloral hydrate I gave you in the powders made you forget. The machine wanted me to forget the small dark man."

"Didn't you ever try to speak to him?" Carr asked. He felt calmer now. Jane's young voice soothed.

"Didn't I tell you how timid I was? I pretended not to notice him. Besides, I knew that strange men who followed girls must never be given a chance of getting them alone. Though I don't think I was ever frightened of him that way. He looked so small and respectul. Actually I suppose I began to feel romantic about him." She took a swallow of her drink.

Carr had finished his. "Well?"

"Oh, he kept coming closer and then one day he walked up and spoke to me. 'Would you mind if I walked with you for a while?' he asked. I gulped and managed to say, 'No.' That's all. He just walked along beside me. It was a long while before he even touched my arm. But that didn't matter. It was what he said that was important. You'll never believe the thrill it gave me. He talked very quietly, rather hesitatingly, but everything he said went straight to my heart. He knew the thoughts inside me I'd never told anyone—how mysterious and puzzling life was, how alone you felt, how other people sometimes seemed just like animals or machines, how dead and menacing their eyes were. And he knew the little things in my mind too—how the piano keys looked like champing teeth, how common words came to be just queer artistic designs, how snores at night sounded like far-away railroad trains and railroad trains like snores. Of course now I know that it was rather easy for him to guess those things, partly because he knew we were both outside the life-machine, even though I didn't.

"After we had walked for a while the first day I saw two of my girl friends ahead. He said, 'I'll leave you now,' and I got that queer blinking feeling and he went off. I was glad, because I wouldn't have known how to introduce him.

"That first walk set a pattern. We'd always meet and part in the same way. And I still had the oddest trouble remembering him and of course I never mentioned him to a soul. Away from the park I'd say, 'You dreamed him, Jane', almost meaning it. But the next afternoon I'd go to the park and he'd appear and I'd walk with him and have the feeling of a friend seeing into my mind. It went on that way for quite a while."

Carr got up and took her glass. He noticed that one of the window shades had about an inch of blackness under it and he went over and pulled it down to the sill.

"And then things changed?" He asked as he made more drinks.

"In a way."

"Did he start to make love to you?"

"No. Perhaps he should have. Perhaps things would have been better if he had. But he couldn't. Because, you see, he was trying to do a very difficult and delicate thing. He wanted me to exist both inside the life-machine and out of it at the same time, without my knowing it. Away from the park I'd just be part of the machine, going through the required motions in a sort of trance. Then at the park with him, I'd break the pattern, but without spoiling the pattern of the rest of my life. Because at the park I'd have just been wandering by myself most of the time, and if he saw I was about to meet someone else, bringing me back into the pattern, he could always drift off.

"He wanted me for a friend, because he was all alone, but he didn't want me alone with him in his dangerous existence, where he'd have to be responsible for me.

"All this meant that he had to be very careful about our meetings and I'd have to be careful about them too.

He made me understand, though he didn't exactly say so, that our walks together were governed by magic rules and everything would be spoiled if they were once broken. For instance, I must never hurry to meet him. It must always happen as if by accident. We must never try to go any special place together. We must talk as familiarly as the closest friends and yet never ask each other our names, and he must always leave me without warning and without arranging when or where we were to meet again. As if everything happened by a quiet, fatalistic enchantment.

"Actually he was trying to drift along beside a part of my life's pattern, an unknown intruder, while I was to be his dream-child, or dream-love, you might say, whom he had awakened, but left entranced in the pattern of her old life, not really changed.

"But he couldn't do it. Not for long. As it turned out, things had to change. No matter how hard he tried, he couldn't conceal from me that there was something horribly important behind what was happening so idly. I sensed a terrible, mute tension inside him. Even when his voice was gentlest and most impersonal I could feel that seething flood of energy, locked up, frustrated, useless. Eventually it began to seep over into me. We'd be walking along slowly and for no good reason my heart would begin to pound. I could hardly breathe, there'd be a ringing in my ears, and little spasms of tension would race up and down me. And all the while he'd be talking ever so calmly. It was awful.

"Perhaps if he had made love to me . . . though of course that would have spoiled his whole plan, and, from his point of view, exposed me to dangers that he didn't feel he had a right to make me share. Still, perhaps if he'd have spoken to me frankly, told me exactly how things were, asked me to share his miserable, hunted life with him, it would have been better.

"But he didn't. And then things began to get much worse."

Carr gave her another drink. "How do you mean?"

Jane looked up at him. Now that she was caught up in her story, she looked younger than ever, and the unevenly blond hair, heavy lipstick, and tight black dress seemed ludicrous, as if she'd fixed herself that way for an adolescent joke.

"We were stuck, that's what it amounted to, and we began to rot. I suppose that's the meaning of decadence—

it never springs from action but from avoiding action. At any rate, all those things he said, that had at first delighted me because they matched my thoughts, now began to terrify me. Because you see, I believed that those queer thoughts of mine were just quirks of my mind, and that by sharing them with someone I'd get rid of them. I kept waiting for him to tell me how silly and baseless they were. But he never did. Instead, I began to see from the way he talked that my queer thoughts weren't illusions at all, but the ultimate truth about the real world. Nothing did mean anything. Snores actually were a kind of engine-puffing and printed words had no more real meaning than wind-tracings in sand. Other people weren't' alive, really alive, like you were, except perhaps for a few ghostlike kindred souls. You were all alone.

"I had discovered his great secret, you see, in spite of all his attempts to hide it from me. Though I didn't tell him that I knew.

"Now the walks in the park did begin to affect the rest of my life. Not so much as to change its pattern, of course, but its moods. All day I'd be plunged in gloom. My father and mother seemed a million miles away, my classes at the academy the most unbearable stupidity in the world. I couldn't read books although I studied the words ever so closely. I didn't understand some of the things I said, the mere appearance of a building or street could frighten me, and sometimes in the middle of my practicing I'd snatch my hands away as if the keys had bitten me. Though, as I say, this didn't change the pattern of my life and of course no one noticed—how could they, parts of a machine in a machine-world?—except Gigolo my cat."

She looked at Carr strangely. "Some animals are really alive, you know, just like some people. Perhaps they catch it from the people. They look at you when you're outside the pattern, and then you know."

"I know," said Carr. "Gigolo looked at me once."

"And not only cats," Jane said.

"What do you mean?" Carr asked uneasily. He had remembered Miss Hackman's references to "the beast."

"Nothing in particular," Jane said after a moment. Carr didn't tell her his thoughts.

"Anyway," Jane continued, "Gigolo knew. Sometimes he acted afraid and spat at me, and sometimes he came purring to me in a most affectionate way—then sometimes he watched at the windows and doors for hours, as if he were on guard. I was lost and not one soul tried to save me, not even my man in the park. He, in a way, least of all—because I think he realized the change in me, but still wanted to save his pleasant dream."

She took a drink and leaned back. "And then one autumn day when the clouds were low and the fallen leaves crackled under our feet, and we'd walked farther together than ever before, in fact, for once he'd come with me a little way out of the park, and I was pleased at that—well, just then I happened to look across the street and I noticed a spruce young man looking at us. That made me glad too, for it was the first time I remembered anyone seeming to look at both of us together, and I was always hoping now that something would break in on us and get us unstuck. I called my friend's attention to the young man. He peered around through his thick glasses.

"The next minute he had grabbed me tight above the elbow and was marching me ahead. He didn't speak until we got around the corner. Then he said, in a voice I'd never heard him use before, 'They've seen us. Get home.'

"I started to ask questions, but he only said, 'Don't talk. Go on quickly. Don't look back.' He said it in such a fierce strange way that I was frightened and obeyed him.

"In the hours afterwards my fear grew. I pictured 'them' in a hundred horrible ways—if only he'd said more than that one word! I dimly sensed that I had transgressed an awful barrier and I felt a terrible guilt. I went to sleep praying never to see the small dark man again and just be allowed to live my old stupid life the way I was meant to live it.

"Some time after midnight I awoke with my heart jumping, and there was Gigolo standing on the bedclothes, spitting at the window. I snapped on the light and it showed me, pressed to the dark pane, the smiling face of the young man I'd seen across the street that afternoon. You know him, Carr. The one they call Dris—Driscoll Aimes. He had two hands then. He used them to open the window."

Carr looked around the room. He leaned forward.

"I jumped up and ran to my father's and mother's room. I called to them to wake up. I shook them. And then came the most terrible shock of my life. They wouldn't wake, no matter what I did. Except that they breathed, they might have been dead. I remember pound-

143

ing my father's chest and digging my nails into his arms.

"I knew then what I'd half guessed for some time—that most people weren't really alive, but only smaller machines in a bigger one. They couldn't understand you, they couldn't help you. If the pattern called for sleep, they slept, and you couldn't do anything about it.

"Sometimes I think that even without Gigolo's warning snarl and the sound of footsteps coming swiftly through the bathroom, I would have rushed out of the apartment, rather than stay a moment longer with those two living corpses who had brought me into the world."

Her voice was getting a little high.

"I darted down the stairs, out of the entry, and into the arms of two other people who were waiting there. You know them, Carr—Miss Hackman and Mr. Wilson. But there was something they hadn't counted on. Gigolo had raced down the stairs with me and with a squalling cry he shot past my legs and sprang into the air between them, seeming to float on the darkness. It must have rattled them, for they drew back and I managed to dart past them and run down the street. I ran several blocks, turning corners, cutting across lawns, before I dared stop. In fact I only stopped because I couldn't run any farther. But it was enough. I had lost them.

"But what was I to do? There was I in the streets in just my nightdress. It was cold. The windows peered. The streetlights whispered. The shadows pawed me. There was always someone crossing a corner two blocks away. I thought of my closest friend, a girl who was at any rate a little closer to me than the others, a girl named Margaret who was studying at the academy. Once in a while I'd gone out with her and her boy-friend. Surely Margaret would take me in, I told myself, surely Margaret would be alive.

"She lived in a duplex just a few blocks from our apartment. Keeping away from the streetlights as much as I could, I hurried over it.

"Her bedroom window was open. I threw some pebbles at it, but nothing happened. I didn't like to ring. Finally by climbing up on the porch I managed to step from it to her window and crawl inside. She was asleep, breathing easily.

"By this time I was trying to tell myself that my father and mother had somehow been drugged as part of a plan to kidnap me. But not for long.

144

"For you see, I was no more able to rouse Margaret than my parents.

"I dressed in some of her clothes and climbed out the window and walked the streets until morning.

"When morning came I tried to go home, but I went carefully and cautiously, spying out my way, and that was lucky, for sitting in a parked automobile not half a block from our door, was Mr. Wilson. I went to the academy and saw Miss Hackman standing at the head of the steps. I went to the park and there, where my small dark man used to wait for me, was Dris.

"That's all. Since then I've lived as you know."

She slumped back in her chair, breathing heavily, still knitting her fingers.

"But I don't know," Carr objected.

"You know enough. I stole my food. I stole other things. Shall I tell you about my shoplifting? Shoplifting from necessity? Shoplifting for fun? And shoplifting just to keep from going crazy? I stole my sleeping places too. Remember that boarded-up mansion I led you to the first night? I sometimes slept there. I made myself a kind of home on the third floor. And then there was a place on the south side, a queer old castle designed by some crazy millionaire, with cement towers and a sunken garden and theosophical inscriptions and ironwork in mystic designs, all abandoned half-built and fenced with rusty wire. And sometimes I slept in the stacks of the library and places like that. Just an outcast, a waif in the life-machine. Oh, Carr, you can't imagine . . . yes, perhaps now you can . . . how utterly alone I was."

He nodded. "Still, at least there was one person," he said slowly "The small dark man."

"That's right. There was Fred. We did happen to meet again."

"I suppose you lived together?" Carr asked softly.

She looked at him. "No we didn't. He helped me find places to live, and we'd meet here and there, and he taught me how to play chess—we played for hours and hours—but I never lived with him."

Carr hesitated. "But surely he must have tried to make love to you," he said. "I know what you told me about him, but after you had run away and there were only two of you together, outcasts, waifs . . ."

She looked down at the floor. "You're right," she said, uncomfortably. "He did try to make love to me."

"And you didn't reciprocate?"

"No."

"Don't be angry with me, Jane, but under the circumstances that seems strange. After all, you have only each other."

She laughed unhappily.

"Oh, I would have reciprocated," she said, "except for one thing, something I found out about him. I don't like to talk about it, but I suppose I'd better. A few weeks after I ran away and we met again—now both of us knowing where we stood—we had an appointment to meet in another park. I came on him unawares and found him holding a little girl. She hardly seemed conscious of him. She was standing there, flushed from running, her bright eyes on her playmates, about to rush off and join them, and he was sitting on the bench behind her, and he had his arms around her, stroking her, tenderly, but with a look in his eyes as if she were so much wood. Sacred wood, perhaps, but wood." Jane sucked in her breath. "Another time I watched him on the outside stairs of an apartment, late at night. There was a young woman beside him, a rather flashily dressed girl. I'd been supposed to meet him but was late. He didn't see me. I watched him from the shadows. He had his hand on her breasts. After a moment she went inside, and he went in with her. But all that time he didn't look once at her face, and his hand kept moving slowly. After that I couldn't bear to have him touch me. In spite of his gentleness and courtesy and understanding, there was a part of him that wanted to take advantage of the life-machine for his private, cold satisfaction—take advantage of the poor dead mechanisms merely because he was aware and they weren't—take advantage in the way those others take advantage. You've seen it in their eyes, haven't you, Carr—Miss Hackman's, Dris's, Mr. Wilson's—that desire to degrade, to play like gods—devils, rather—with the poor earthly puppets? Well, there was a small part of Fred that was like them." She hesitated. "Even then I might have yielded if he hadn't approached me in such a guilty way."

"Wait . . . The child in the park. Was she aware of him?"

"I think so. A little, anyway. As the animals are. She was not in fear. Just puzzled, at first. Then the little girl seemed to experience a kind of strange shuddering ec-

146

stasy. Not her own. *His* ecstasy reflected in her. And not just simply physical ecstasy of the perverted kind which can be comprehended even if abhorred—but a mental thing, a cruel perversion of the mind. The perversion of power—"

"And the woman, what about her?"

"She seemed unaware that she was being—loved. Physically, by someone. But there was a wickedly ecstatic look to her, as if she were dreaming some deep evilness."

"Huh . . . Nice guy!"

"Understand," she went on hurriedly, "the rest of him was really fine—the most comradely sympathy, the highest ideals. He even had, I think, the quixotic notion that he wouldn't be worthy of me until he had somehow rescued me and returned me to my safe life again."

"But that's impossible," Carr interrupted, looking at Jane dully, "Once you're outside the pattern—" (As he uttered those words he felt well up within him the longing of a living man for a once meaningful world, now forever meaningless) "—how can you ever get back?"

"Oh, but you can," Jane said quickly. "You were back in the pattern, conscious but a part of it, from the time I gave you the powders until you ran away from that party. Even without drugs, it can be done. You're born with a feeling for the rhythm of life as the machine wants it. You learn to sense it. You automatically do and say what you're supposed to. You can—"

The phone rang. For a moment they both sat very still. Carr looked at Jane. Then he slowly reached over and lifted the phone from the cradle. As he did so, the familiarity of the action took possession of him, drawing him back without his realization toward the pattern of his old life.

"That you, Carr?"

"Yes."

"This is Tom."

"Hello, Tom."

"Look, have you anything on for the night after to-morrow?"

"Why . . . no." Carr caught his breath in surprise. Only now did he realize that he had been answering automatically. He was talking to a machine, he reminded himself —a machine to which dates, and girls and words and all the rest of it, were only a mechanical function.

147

"Swell. How about coming dancing with the three of us?"

"Who do you mean?" (Still, to Carr's amazement, his answers came almost without his bidding.)

"You know, Midge's girl-friend."

"Midge's girl-friend?"

"Sure, you know—I've told you about her half a dozen times."

"I remember," Carr said.

"Well, are you coming?" (There suddenly seemed to be a phonograph sound, a machine chug, in the voice coming over the phone.)

Carr hesitated. "I don't know." (How was he supposed to answer, he asked himself?)

"Oh, for God's sake!" (Again the machine-chug.)

Still Carr hesitated, painfully. Then, "Well, okay," he said. (That was the answer that felt right to him.)

"You don't sound very enthusiastic." (It had been right!)

"No, it's okay. I'll come."

"Swell. We'll pick you up at about seven."

Car frowned at the phone wonderingly as he put it down.

"You see," Jane told him, "you were part of the pattern then, right back in it, and your answers came naturally. Incidently, you made a date with me."

Carr's head swiveled around. He stared at her. "What!"

Jane nodded. "You did. Tom's girl Midge is that Margaret I told you about. Which makes me Midge's girl-friend. That's how I happened to know about General Employment and why I ran in there when I was trying to deceive Miss Hackman. I would have gone to Tom's desk, except you happened to be the one who didn't have an applicant, so by going to you I could make Miss Hackman think I was in the pattern. And then it turned out that you weren't part of the pattern, and still you helped me."

Carr looked at her wonderingly. It was very quiet.

"I wish we could keep that date you just made," she said. "I wish we could go back to our old lives, now that our meeting there is part of the pattern."

"Why can't we?" Carr asked suddenly. He leaned forward and caught her hand. "You say it's possible to de-

148

velop a feel for the pattern, to live according to it even though you're aware."

"You're forgetting those others," she reminded him. "They know my place in the pattern. I hope not, but they may guess yours. They're watching. They'd know if I went back. And then they'd destroy me. For nothing will ever satisfy them, until . . ."

At that moment they heard a step on the stairs.

Carr plunged the room into darkness. Jane came to him and they clung silently together, facing the door. No cracks of light showed around it. The burnt-out light-bulb in the hall had not been replaced.

The steps came closer. A faint and shifting light began to show through the cracks.

It is frightful to be in a deserted house. Even if the outdoors were a wilderness, its air would still carry that promise of other lives, which the walls of the deserted house bar out.

But to be in such a house and hear alien footsteps, and know that outside is a deserted city, where the men and women might be wax figures for all the help they could give you, and to know that beyond the deserted city is a deserted world, a deserted universe . . .

The footsteps stopped outside the door. There was a soft knocking. Carr's hands tightened on Jane's. A pause. The knocking was repeated, louder. Another pause. Again the knocking, louder yet.

A longer pause. Then a faint scratching that lasted for some time. Then a brief rustling.

Then the footsteps and light going away. Down the hall. Down the stairs. Silence.

Carr and Jane swayed. Their breath came in gasps. Carr went to the windows, pulled the drapes too, so that they formed a second barrier behind the shades. Then he struck a match, cupping it in his hand. It flared red, then yellow.

Janet said, "Look."

Thrust under the bottom of the door was a folded sheet of paper.

Carr picked it up. He struck another match. They read the hastily scribbled note.

My Angry Passenger,
    If you possibly can, meet me tomorrow eve-

149

ning at seven in front of the public library. Bring Jane, if you know where she is. I've made a very important discovery.

Your Mad Chauffeur

CHAPTER THIRTEEN

The Black Shape

FROM BEHIND THE castellated black wall of warehouses, elevators, bridges, and cranes to the west, the setting sun sent a giant spray of dark red fire streaming through the immensity of air above the Chicago River. It bloodily edged the giant shoulders of the skyscrapers crowded around the Michigan Avenue bridge like a herd of gray mammoths stopping by the river for the night. It glared from their many faceted window-eyes to the west, but left those to the east in gloom—the small, wickedly intelligent window-eyes expressing the hard, alien thoughts that cities have been thinking since Ur and Alexandria and Rome. It turned the white tiles of the Wrigley Tower a delicate salmon pink and the golden trim of the Carbon and Carbide Building a rosy copper.

Far below the crimson light glimmered on the river, ruddily touched a black motor-barge, gleamed and faintly glittered on the asphalt and cement of the street bordering the river and the huge bridge crossing it, but hardly penetrated the dark rectangles below that were the windows to the bridge below the bridge, the street below the street —that cobbled and concrete underworld of rumbling trucks and parked cars, of coal-dust and dirt, with its own scattering of blinking and neon signs, that lay beneath the northern end of Chicago's Loop district.

The same light struck color from the dresses, lost itself in the dark suits, of the streams of figures that moved like tired ants across the upper bridge, the purposeless, irregular cavalcade of tiny figures made tinier and more purposeless yet by the great buildings lowering above them.

150

In the heart of this throng, Carr and Jane drifted. Around them, shoulders and elbows eddied, meaningless voices swirled on the deeper currents of sound from the trucks and cars. Occasionally the stream whirled by them a briefcase or a parasol.

They were carried across the bridge and down the deep canyon beyond, past the black stairheads leading down to the lower-level streets at block intervals. They kept their eyes from the faces of figures around them, though Carr couldn't help but notice certain oddities, such as a smoking bus with the crowd piling out of it, the figure of a man with a sandwich board, and the shape of a woman leading a large and ungainly black dog.

Finally they fronted the dark headland of the public library. Here they turned their faces toward each other, as two divers might before the plunge.

They moved closer to each other, arm locking arm, hand grasping hand. Then they turned their faces forward and crossed the street. Here the crowd, augmented by streams seeking the Illinois Central pedestrian underpass, was thicker. The figure of the woman with the queer black dog was just ahead. They had taken about a dozen steps when a gap chanced to appear in the mass of bodies ahead of them, letting them look down a rather long corridor of empty sidewalk. Carr felt Jane's hand loosen on his, then tighten sharply.

Standing at the other end of the momentary corridor, facing them, was the small dark man with glasses.

He saw them and smiled fantastically. Yielding to an impulse deeper than caution, he raised his hand in a theatrical gesture of greeting.

But then his glance shifted, shortened. He recoiled. His thick glasses flashed as his head jerked back. He clapped his hands to his chest, arms tight against his ribs, as if to protect his heart. Then, as the corridor which chance had brought into existence began swiftly to narrow, he looked again at Carr and Jane with a crouched frantic intentness.

Then, just as the corridor ahead closed, he cried out unintelligibly, bounded into the air like a puppet, and raced off.

Instantly three other figures detached themselves from the intervening crowd and ran after him. Two were men. The third was the woman with the dog.

Without a word, Carr and Jane started after them, stepping faster, faster, faster, until they were running too.

Over heads and through holes in the crowd, Carr saw snatches of the chase—the small dark man weaving and ducking as he sought gaps in the crowd, every few steps taking one of those incredible bounds, the three pursuers sprinting after him.

The crowd did not react. No eyes turned, no people sprang aside, no shouts went up, no heads were poked from windows. Even the figures being darted and ducked around, missing being knocked down by inches—they never turned a hair, they went on smiling as sweetly, chattering as vivaciously, and peering as guardedly at good-looking young women, as if nothing had ruffled the charm of the afternoon.

Carr ran faster. The glimpse he caught showed him that the small dark man was holding his own, even beginning to gain. They had passed the library and were in the next block.

Then he saw Mr. Wilson motion urgently to Miss Hackman. She checked her pace and stopped, so that crowd cut off Carr's view of her.

A moment later there was a shape taking great effortless bounds—a coal-black wolfish shape that still carried the suggestion of the feline.

The small dark man looked back once, thrust up from the crowd like a hand puppet. Then he ran frantically a few steps farther and darted into a haberdashery store.

The black shape was at his heels.

One second, two, three—then from the store began to come shrill screams of terror and agony that sliced the heart.

Carr felt a great wave of nausea. Here, he saw in an unwilling flash of thought, was an allegory of the universe's whole history—those screams crying out death and horror and pain, a murderer loose in the house of life, catlike cruelty at the cosmos' core, destruction holding a match to the earth's fuse—and the machine-men going about their patterned business with their minds black, their eyes blind, their ears unhearing.

The screams stopped.

Dris, Miss Hackman, and Mr. Wilson reached the store and hurried inside.

Miss Hackman came out after a moment. Her feet dragged. She was looking at the sidewalk. Her complexion wasn't good. Carr and Jane could see her stomach suddenly jerk in and her shoulders heave forward.

152

The black shape came out and rubbed against her affectionately, and now Carr recognized it. It was a black cheetah. Miss Hackman averted her eyes and flopped her hand at it. It persisted. She walked off toward the next corner, away from Jane and Carr. She had her hand to her mouth. The black cheetah followed, muzzling her ankles.

Red blotches appeared on her stockings.

Jane and Carr began to back away.

Mr. Wilson come out of the store. He looked around. He saw Miss Hackman and hurried after her.

Carr and Jane continued to back away. They passed a series of chromium fitted windows, recrossed the street behind them, started back along the library. The sidewalk crowd, a minute before so thick, had now thinned disturbingly.

Mrs. Wilson caught up with Miss Hackman. She stopped. He seemed to be expostulating with her and she to be nodding her head abjectly.

"We'll cut over to the Loop at the next corner," Carr whispered. Jane nodded.

They turned and walked swiftly along the blank wall of rough stone beneath the library's recessed windows. They had almost reached the corner when a bus drew up at it and a crowd of sailors came whooping out, their legs working like blue scissors. Carr had fallen back a little. Just as Jane went around the corner the sailors cut in between them. Before he pushed through he took one last backward look.

Driscoll Aimes wasn't more than thirty feet behind him, stepping along briskly. He saw Carr just as Carr saw him. For a moment he stood stock-still. Then he came on with a rush.

Carr turned and ran across the street, straight up Michigan Boulevard, praying that Jane would keep on going and escape notice.

The bright-eyed, sulky-lipped mannequins in the dress shops were more alive than the people around whom he swerved and dodged.

He looked back. He had gained on Driscoll Aimes, who was running easily. And—thank God!—Jane wasn't in sight.

Carr darted down the iron stairs into the dimness of the lower-level street. The tread clanged under his feet.

Once underground, he kept on running in the same direction. The sidewalk here was about five feet above the

153

cobbled street, level with the tops of the cars parked side by side in a continuous row. At intersections it descended by steps and ascended again. Two blocks ahead, rectangular windows of twilight indicated the embankment and the river.

At the end of the last block, Carr darted another backward look. Dris was not in sight, but, bounding along the tops of the parked cars, as if their painted metal were a more congenial surface to its feet than the concrete of the sidewalk, came the black cheetah.

Carr remembered the screams that had come from the haberdashery.

He plunged down the last steps, darted in front of a truck that dribbled ashes, and sprinted toward the embankment. Behind him he could hear a rythmical padding.

He burst into the twilight of the embankment.

Without checking his pace, he crossed it and dove toward the oily water.

He had a glimpse of black pilings rushing by. His head was struck a heavy blow. There was a rush of pain.

He was conscious of the coldness of the water, of the weight of his clothes, of fading light, of nothingness.

CHAPTER FOURTEEN

The Cleared Vision

FIRST THERE WAS a throbbing. Then the throbbing split into two parts: pain and a slow rocking. Then several sensations: The reek of burning oil and water-rotted wood. The feel of blankets against naked skin. A swaying light. A low ceiling. A general ache. A faint nausea.

Then the realization that all this centered in one person and that person was himself.

Then a great misty oval above him that slowly unblurred into a face. A huge pale face with wide heavy jaws that suggested glandular disfunction. A wide mouth with pendant underlip and yellowed teeth. Heavily

154

seamed cheeks, a bashed-in nose, cavernous eye-sockets with large unwinking eyes, the whites faintly muddied. Tufty black eyebrows shot with gray. Above, a great white dome of forehead. The expression was one of brooding solicitude.

Carr felt a big hand under his shoulders lifting him effortlessly. A thick glass was gently pushed against his lips. "Here."

It was whisky and water. Carr drank it in small swallows. Then he looked at the face again. He recognized the giant bargeman who had once looked up at him on the bridge. He guessed he was in the cabin of the black motor-barge.

But he didn't want to think. It wasn't the pain so much as a general sick listlessness. He was content to lie back in the blankets.

The bargeman stood up. He was so tall that in spite of his stooping his head barely missed the small, curved beams that supported the roof of the cabin, and from one of which a flaring oil lamp hung.

"You'll live, all right," he said in a rumbling voice. "Though I wouldn't have sworn to it when I fished you out. How'd you get in that fix anyway? Who was it you bothered? I suppose you went around stirring things up, like most of the other fools. The gang don't like that. It spoils their show. You ought to learn to live quiet, like I do." And he reached out a big splay-fingered hand and poured himself a drink of whisky in the tumbler from which Carr had drunk.

The paint on the walls was blackened and peeling. At the far end was a small cookstove, a pantry, a sink, and a rusty watertank bracketed to the ceiling. At the same height were several ventilation slits but Carr couldn't see out of them. He noticed his clothes drying on a short washline. Opposite the bunk was a wide sliding door, shut. There were several chests and boxes about. Next to the door was a bookcase made of fruit crates. It was packed with thick volumes. Tacked to the wall wherever space allowed were pictures of prizefighters, cut from newspapers, and cheap reproductions of engravings and etchings by Dore and Goya.

The bargeman poured himself another drink of whisky and sat down in a gray unpainted chair. He scratched the hair on his chest where it brushed out around his undershirt. He frowned at Carr.

"How'd you catch on, anyway?" He sat forward, elbows on knees. "Most folks don't, you know. They can't."

He paused, as if to let his words sink in. Then, "It happened to *me* pretty sudden," he continued. "My name's Jules. Old Jules. I used to be a sailor, but I liked to think. I'd go to one of the big libraries and make them get me all sorts of books. Philosophy, metaphysics," he split the syllables carefully, "science, even a little religion, I'd read in them and try to figure out the world. What was it all about, anyway? Why was I here? What was the point in the whole business of getting born and working and dying? What was the use of it? Why'd it have to go on and on?

"And why'd it have to be so damn complicated? Why all the building and tearing down? Why'd there have to be cities, with crowded streets and busses and cable cars and electric cars and big openwork steel boxes built to the sky to be hung with stone and wood—my only friend got killed falling off one of those steel boxkites. Shouldn't there be some simpler way of doing it all? Why did things have to be so mixed up that a man like myself couldn't have a single clear decent thought?"

Carr listened dreamily. The whisky was taking effect. His head didn't ache so badly now.

"More'n that, why weren't people a real part of the world?" the other continued, taking a gulp of whisky from the glass. "Why didn't they show more honest-to-God response? Yes, that was it—response. For instance, when you slept with a woman, why was it something you had, and she didn't? Why, when you went to a prize fight, were the bruisers only so much meat, and the crowd a lot of little screaming popinjays? Why was a war nothing but marching and blather and bother? Why'd everybody have to go through their whole lives so dead, doing everything so methodical and prissy, like they was a Sunday School picnic or an orhpan's parade?"

He rubbed the back of his neck and pulled his chair a little closer.

"And then all of a sudden, when I was reading one of the science books, it come to me. The answer was all there, printed out plain to see, only nobody could see it. It was just this: *Nobody was really alive.* Back of other people's foreheads there wasn't any real thoughts . . . just nerves, just wheels. You didn't need thoughts or minds, or love or fear, to explain things. The whole universe—

156

stars and men and dirt and worms and atoms, the whole shooting match—was just one great big engine."

He finished his drink.

Carr turned his head a little so that he could see the bargeman more clearly. It almost soothed him to hear the horrors of the last few days spoken out so casually.

"So there it was all laid out for me," the bargeman continued. "That was why there was no honest-to-God response in people. They were just machines. The fighters was just machines made for fighting. The people that watched them was just machines for stamping and screaming and swearing. A woman was just a loving machine, all nicely adjusted to give you a good time . . . but the farthest star was nearer to you than the mind behind that mouth you kissed.

"D'ja get what I mean? People just machines, set to do a certain job and then die. If you kept on being the machine you were supposed to be, well and good. Then your actions fitted with other people's. But if you didn't, if you started doing something else, then the others didn't respond. They just went on doing what was called for. It wouldn't matter what you did, they'd just go on making the motions they were set to make. They might be set to make love, and you might decide you wanted to fight. Then they'd go on making love while you fought them. Or it might happen the other way. Somebody might be talking about Edison. And you'd happen to say something about Ingersoll. But he'd just go on talking about Edison. You were all alone!"

He slewed around in his chair and poured himself another whisky.

"All alone. Except for a few others—not more than one in a hundred thousand, I guess—who wake up and figure things out. But they go crazy and run themselves to death, or else turn mean. Mostly they turn mean. They get a cheap little kick out of pushing things around that can't push back. All over the world you'll find them— little gangs of three or four, half a dozen—who've waked up, just to their cheap kicks. Maybe it's a couple of coppers in Frisco, a schoolteacher in K.C., some artists in New York, some rich kids in Florida, some undertakers in London—who've found out that all the people walking around are just dead folks and to be treated no decenter. Maybe it's a couple of guards over at one of those death-camps they had in Europe, who see how bad things are and get their fun out of making it a little worse. Just a little. A mean little. They don't dare to really destroy in a big way, because they know the machine feeds them and tends them, and because they're always scared they'll be noticed by gangs like themselves and wiped out; It's fear drives them, always fear. They haven't the guts to really wreck the whole shebang, but they get a kick out of scribbling their dirty pictures on it, out of meddling and messing with it. I've seen some of their fun, as they call it, sometimes hidden away, sometimes in the open streets. It's lousy and rotten.

"You've seen a clerk dressing a figure in a store window, fiddling around with it? Well, suppose he slapped its face. Suppose a kid struck pins in a toy pussy-cat, or threw pepper in the eyes of a doll. Like that. Lousy and rotten. No decent live man would have anything to do with it. He'd either go back to his place in the machine and act out the part set for him, or else he'd hide away like me and live as quiet as he could, not stirring things up."

He looked at Carr from under his arched and ragged brows. "What are *you* going to do? You're young. Why don't you go back to your place in the machine and sweat it out that way?"

Carr tried to lift himself up a little. The room rocked and blurred. "I can't," he heard himself whispering, "because the ones after me know my place. And there's a girl. They know her place too . . . if they haven't found her already."

The bargeman leaned forward, elbows on knees. "Who are they?" he asked. "What gang? What do they look like?"

Carr heard himself describing Miss Hackman, Mr. Wilson, and Driscoll Aimes. When he was part way through, the bargeman interrupted him.

"I know them. A mean lot. I've seen that bitchy black cat of theirs."

He slopped the rest of the whisky into his tumbler, drank, then sat working his big-knuckled hands. Finally he heaved himself up. The tumbler rolled across the floor. He lurched to the door, slid it open wide. The darkness and the noises of the city flowed in. He looked around.

"You go back," he mumbled at Carr. "You and your girl go on back. Don't worry about anything. Leave it to me, leave it to Old Jules. I got connections." He flapped his big hand at Carr. "You go back." Then he stumbled through the door and slid it to behind him.

Carr sat up, biting his lips against the sudden rush of dizziness. He got his legs over the edge of the bunk and sat there, the cool air drifting along his skin, the walls of the cabin advancing and retreating and every now and then erupting in a corruscation of bright sparks.

After a while he stood up, holding on to the edge of the bunk. As soon as his eyes quieted down he made his way across the cabin, remembering to stoop, until his fingers reached his clothes where they were hanging, stiff from the water. He dressed slowly and clumsily like a child. His trousers were stuck together and he had to run his hands down the legs.

He heard the distant hooting of a ship on the lake. He finished dressing and stood smoothing his clothes. Then he made his way to the door, with difficulty slid it open, and stepped out onto the narrow deck.

The late night-sounds of Chicago enfolded him—the lonesome purr of traffic, the jangling of a bell, the rattle of an elevated train crossing the Wells Street bridge, the rumble of unidentified machinery. Across the river, Carr saw three or four sets of headlights probing their way along the two levels of Wacker Drive, a red warning light on the embankment, a few patches of lighted window in the towering buildings, and their reflections wriggling like quicksilver on the black water.

Carr realized that the barge was moored to the embankment. Only he was standing on the side of the barge away from it. With groggy care he made his way around the deck, by the stern, found the embankment, peered over the rail, saw hardly a foot of water between him and the stone. He waited a moment, got his legs over the rail, steadied himself.

Just then a great red glow flamed up behind him, turning the nearer bricks of the embankment bright almost as day. Clutching the rail spasmodically, pressing his legs against it to steady himself, Carr turned his head. He saw the bargeman standing at the prow with a railroad flare sizzling in his hand. Against the black river, the lower half of his huge body cut off by the low cabin, his back in the shadow, his lumpy muscles and great face and tangled hair reflecting the blinding red light, he looked like some torchbearer in the inferno, some signalman on the styx. He saw Carr. Seven times he whirled the torch in a circle, then seven times more, then he sent it whirling high in the air.

"Signals," he muttered enigmatically across the cabin. "Trust Old Jules."

The flare shot down like a small meteor, hissed out in the river.

"Listen!" Carr heard the bargeman call. He could hardly see him for the moment, the darkness swam so after the flare, or else his dizziness had come back. "Listen! D'ya hear it?" the bargeman repeated in a hushed and drunken voice. Carr strained his ears but was aware of nothing but the machine-sounds of Chicago. "There it is," the bargeman called, "Clankety-clank . . . clankety-clank . . . That's the real sound of the universe. That's the music of the spheres. That's your heavenly choir. Not very sweet is it?" He paused. Then turning toward the city, he shook his fist. "But you wait," he roared, "you wait! Your time's coming. There's a new power running the big engine. A power that can melt cities like a blow-torch melts steel. We'll see if the big engine can stand up under that, and people still all asleep. We'll see! We'll see! We'll see!"

Carr's vision cleared. He stepped across the ribbon of water and walked unsteadily up the embankment.

CHAPTER FIFTEEN

Quiet, Daisy

CARR OPENED THE door of his apartment, steadied himself against the frame. The windows were still black with night. He softly called, "Jane?" There was no answer. He slumped a little. His head felt painful, his body fagged, his clothes wretchedly uncomfortable.

He listened to the faint, throaty machine-hum of 4 A.M. Chicago, like the purring of a circle of vast, crouching cats. He shivered. Then he gathered himself together, shut the door and switched on the light.

He glanced at the letter he had automatically snatched from his pigeon-hole downstairs. It was from Marcia. No need to look at that one. He had read it—let's see—two nights ago. He tossed it down.

A propped rectangle of paper on the mantle caught his eye. There were only a few lines of writing on it. His chest felt tight as he read the signature: "Jane."

The writing was more hurried and crabbed than any of hers he had seen before, but he quickly made it out.

> This place is no longer safe. I've gone to the old mansion, to my place on the third floor. Come to me there.

It seemed to Carr that the distant purring grew a shade more deep and menacing. He went to the bureau, rummaged around, found a flashlight. It made only an old yellow glow, but he stuck it in his pocket.

Outside in the late darkness, the streets were more deserted than he had ever known them. His footsteps seemed to echo for blocks. He felt a vague gratitude toward the chance forces that had made a path for him, that had cleared the way of automatons. For he was fearfully tired. Only the thought that he would soon be with Jane kept him moving. The awful discoveries of the past days weighed on him as crushingly as if his body were a clumsy metal machine that he must hold up with the feeble strength of flesh and sinew. If he could now go back to his appointed place in life, he felt that he would never have more strength than to do merely his machine work. He would be a machine and nothing more than a machine.

If only he and Jane could go back . . . That possibility now seemed to him infinitely desirable, infinitely distant. The drunken words of Old Jules the bargeman repeated themselves in his memory—hollow, remote, a childishly futile challenge to a dead universe.

The blocks dragged slowly by. All that actually seemed to change was the quality of his footsteps' echoes, as they came now from this wall, now that.

The emptiness of the streets was phenomenal. For a while he toyed dully with the notion that Chicago had been emptied of all its automatons, until he passed a single figure in a dark, shiny coat standing by the street car tracks a block from his destination.

Weariness came at him in waves. It occurred to him that although he had only now learned that the universe was a machine, it had always felt like one. His head sagged.

He found his hands loosely circling black wrought iron bars. He gripped them tighter to rouse himself, and looked up. As in a dream, the old mansion showed as a colorless, shadow-wrapped pile in the first paleness of dawn. All the windows were blind, the lower with boards, the upper with jagged edged blackness. As he made his way up the weedy drive, past the old "For Sale" sign, a tiny wind rustled the dark leaves overhead, then died. The odor from the rank garden was bitter and strong.

The big door under the porte-cochere was an inch ajar. He listened for a moment, then pushed at it. It scuffed complainingly across humped-up carpet, as the gate had across gravel.

He stepped inside, and instantly half his weariness dropped away, as if the old house demanded alertness as its due. The odor changed from bitter to musty, with a hint of water-rot. The dingy beam of his flashlight revealed a floor half-carpeted, half bare; walls cobwebbed with soot showing slightly paler rectangles where pictures had once hung; two shapeless bulks of covered chairs; a wide and curving stairway with an elaborately carved, key-thick newel post; several dark, wide doorways.

He glowed his light into the latter openings, revealing more dirt and emptiness and, down the one leading toward the back of the house, the foot of a second and narrower stairway.

He stood just inside the door, conscious of a mounting anxiety. He realized that he was waiting for Jane to call to him, that he had expected his questing flashlight beam to reveal her face. It occurred to him for the first time that it was strange she should arrange to meet him on the third floor, and that she shouldn't call out or come down, now that she must hear him coming.

He crossed to the wider stairway, straining his ears after each step, and started up it. He switched off his flashlight. The treads creaked faintly under his weight. The odor of old dust grew thicker—even his cautious footsteps must be raising puffs of it. He gazed up the oval stairwell at the smaller oval of paler gloom marking the ceiling of the third floor, where the broken windows must be letting in a little light. It seemed to him that the smaller oval

162

showed an irregularity, as if perhaps a head were peering down. But when he moved up another step he could no longer see it.

For some reason, his imagination kept picturing, not Jane, but the figure in the dark raincoat he had passed back by the car tracks. He had hardly glanced at its face, but now he found himself wishing he had, for he was conscious of a belated sense of recognition.

He paused on the second floor landing, then continued up. After six steps he stopped dead.

There could be no mistaking it now. There it thrust above the heavy bannister at the head of the stair, the darkness of a head against the faintly lesser darkness of the wall. The silence seemed to congeal around him as he peered at it.

Suddenly he pointed his flashlight, switched it on. In the yellow circle he saw Jane's face, staring at him in terror.

He called her name, rushed up the last steps. Then they were in each other's arms. Carr felt the last of his weariness vanish, then return momentarily with a rush, so that he swayed at the stair-head, hugging her drunkenly.

"Darling, I was so afraid it wasn't you," she said in a breath, her fingers digging into his shoulders. "Why didn't you call out?"

"I don't know," he answered stupidly. "I was expecting you to."

"But I couldn't be sure it was you," she told him. "Why were you so long? It was waiting here in the dark that frightened me. It's been hours and hours. What happened to you?"

In a few slow sentences he explained why he had run away from her and sketched for her his plunge into the river and rescue by the bargeman.

"Yes, but afterwards?" she pressed. "What did you do afterwards?"

"I came straight here," he told her, "as soon as I got back to my room."

"You couldn't have," she said, stepping back a little. "It's been hours."

"What do you mean?" he asked puzzledly.

"And how did it all happen so quickly?" she continued rapidly. "The business with the bargeman, I mean. It couldn't have been more than half an hour after I lost you by the library that I hurried back to your room, yet when I got there, your note was waiting for me."

He took her arms. The silence of the old house became deadly. *My* note?"

"Yes, telling me to come here and wait for you."

He tried to study her expression in the dark gray light. Under his hands he felt her arms grow rigid, as though his own gathering fear were seeping over into her.

"Jane," he whispered, "I only got back to my room twenty minutes ago. I didn't leave any note. I came here because of yours."

"My . . . ?"

"Your note."

"But, Carr, I didn't . . ." she began. Then he felt her jerk and freeze like a frightened animal.

He heard, in the silence, a faint scuffling sound. Again it came—tight, complaining. He recognized it.

It was the porte-cochere door opening.

Then footsteps in the big hall two flights down.

As if it were some other person speaking, some shadowy other Carr who thought of strategies and tactics while the main Carr was hypnotized by fear, he heard himself whisper, "There's another stairway at the back. We might—"

Just then, like a fantastically amplified echo, the words came booming up from below:

"There's another stairway at the back."

But the tones were the deep, hearty ones of Mr. Wilson.

"*That's* all right." Miss Hackman's happy, strident tones rocketed across his deeper ones. "If they try to use it, Daisy will notice, won't you, dear?"

Carr felt Jane shake spasmodically, then freeze again. He tried to draw her away from the head of the stairs, but she was rigid as a stick. Everything seemed to him to be happening in very slow motion, so that when a third and brisker voice rose up the well, saying, "Let's get busy," the three words came to his ears yards apart. The odor of dust in his nostrils was something to be carefully sensed, precisely examined. In the gathering light he could begin to make out the leaf-and-stem pattern of the wall-paper beyond Jane's head.

There was a medley of steps on the stairs, and mixed with them, a rhythmic and rapid padding. From where he was standing Carr could peer crosswise down the well to a small segment of the first flight of steps, which were still plunged in blackness. But then it seemed to his heightened vision that a brighter, sleeker blackness momentarily flashed there.

Like a puff of cheap perfume, there came up the stairwell the sugarsweet voice of Miss Hackman: "Don't hurry Daisy, there'll be lots of time."

Again Carr tried to draw Jane away. She wouldn't move. Yet he inwardly realized that this attempt on his part was little more than a sham, that the other Carr who tried to think of the defensive possibilities of the broken-windowed rooms around them was getting dimmer and more shadowy every moment. No, this was it. This was the finish for a pair of lovers who had found that life was very much like a night spent on a wager in a waxworks museum with some of the figures finally coming alive. Escape into a dead and shelterless world was futile. He had a momentary vision of the fate of the small dark man with glasses. No, there was nothing to do at all.

Jane was like a statue in his arms, except that he could feel the terrified breaths creep up and down her throat. His mind was curiously empty, concerned with such trivial things as the wall-paper, the light, and the identity of the figure in the dark slicker he had passed by the car tracks. For some reason that question nagged him.

The steps on the stairs slowed.

"Well, they're up there, all right. The hair's broken." Mr. Wilson's words had an eminently businesslike ring, though interspersed with puffing. Then, as the steps came onto the second-story landing, "Wait a minute. I'm out of breath."

"Very well. Down, Daisy." Miss Hackman's voice was amiable.

"Sh! They'll hear you." This time the voice was Dris's.

Miss Hackman dwelt lovingly on her reply, lavishing on it all her sugariness. "I know they will."

Carr studied the pattern of the wallpaper. It seemed to him he could see the light increase by visible stages, like the movements of the minute hand of a watch. He noted a thickening of the musty odor, as if from dust raised by their footsteps.

From the landing below came Mr. Wilson's puffing and a soft and rapid padding back and forth over a very short distance. Carr could picture them clearly, though his paralyzed mind perversely attached much greater importance to the problem of the figure in the dark slicker. Mr.

Wilson seated on the top step, chest heaving, knees drawn up, perhaps carefully holding his coat tails out of the dust. Dris back by the wall, a slim shadow, hand and hook at his sides. Miss Hackman standing with one foot on the top step, one below, leaning forward in some flamboyant suit, elbow on knee, blonde hair dripping around her face, holding in her hand a very short leash at the end of which a brighter, sleeker blackness paced. As they spoke, he could picture their expressions vividly—although the other problem persisted in seeming to him much more important.

"Let's get on," Dris said sharply.

"There's no hurry at all," Miss Hackman assured him. "Quiet, Daisy!"

"Just the same, it would have been simpler to finish them off back there," Dris continued stubbornly.

"And have to spend hours cleaning up the mess?" Miss Hackman's reply was quick and scornful. "Have you forgotten the trouble we had because of the little man with glasses. On your knees for half an hour, scrubbing?"

"You weren't so keen on that business yourself," he told her.

"That didn't happen to strike me. This does. Here we don't have to rush things or worry about cleaning up afterwards." She paused reflectively. "Oh, how stupid of them to let themselves be lured here with those notes," she said gayly. "How stupid of her to think we didn't know she used to come here. How stupid of them both to be so utterly, completely guileless. How stupid of him not to realize we could get his home address at his office. It's almost too easy. Still," she went on thoughtfully, "they're alive, and it's really only live things that are any fun."

"Let's get on," Dris repeated insistently.

"Not by any chance a date? With your girls?"

"Don't be ridiculous. No, I've got a feeling . . . that we're being watched."

"Silly lad." Miss Hackman's voice was wholly happy again. "Of course we are, and listened to, too."

"I don't mean by them," Dris told her.

But Carr was hardly listening to what they said, for he had just recaptured a memory that perversely afforded him a great satisfaction—the identity of the figure in the dark slicker.

It had been one of the men on South State Street who

166

had stood on the curb when he and Jane—and those three —had fled.

"You've a feeling, Dris?" At last Mr. Wilson spoke again, even-breathed, and for once not heartily, instead almost apprehensively.

"Yes."

"Then let's get on with this quickly." The stairs creaked as he heaved up his fat body, the footsteps started again, and there was an eager change in the rhythmic padding, then:

"What's that!" Mr. Wilson almost shouted.

"They're trying for the back stairs," Miss Hackman screeched. "Daisy!"

"No, they're not, you idiot!" Mr. Wilson roared. "I think—"

"I warned you—" Dris began.

"My God, it's—" Mr. Wilson started to say.

But Carr was so preoccupied with his recaptured memory, that at first it seemed to him of no consequence— perhaps just something his sick mind was imagining— when he heard a sudden rush of footsteps on the floor below, more footsteps than those three could make, and in addition coming with a rush from the back of the house and pounding up the stairs from the first floor.

Even when Jane jerked in his arms, when, with shocking loudness in the echoing stair-well, there came the crash of half dozen gunshots, he hardly roused himself fully to what was happening—or rather he realized how what was happening fitted his recaptured memory, how it led from South State Street by the red glare of a railway flare to Old Jules's barge, to the man by the car tracks, and so here.

With Jane rocking wildly in his arms, he heard, as the echoes of the gunfire died, a shrill scream that ended in a gargling groan, thud of a body, a squalling animal scream, a rush of paws, another earsplitting burst of gunfire, thud of another body, one last gunshot, and then the fainter diminishing rhythmic thuds of a body rolling down the stairs, step by step.

Then silence, complete silence, almost more shocking than the noise.

A cloud of acrid smoke mushrooming up the well.

Then, out of the silence below, a voice, unfamiliar, flat, cruel: "Well, that finished them, and in a good spot. Get you bad, George?"

Another unfamiliar voice: "Just a scratch."

A third voice: "Shall we search the rest of the house?"

The first voice, after what seemed to Carr an eternity: "No, there were only these three and the cat when we followed them in. Besides, there were only three in this gang. Old Jules said so."

Footsteps descending the stairs.

Sound of the porte-cochere door closing.

Carr felt Jane twist from his arms. She hurried into the room behind them. He found her peering over the sill through the dirty and half-shattered window. Kneeling cautiously beside her, he got his own eyes up in time to see, going down the weedy driveway in the chilly light, a half-dozen men in dark slickers.

They crouched there at the window. The driveway emptied. The light was enough now so that the weeds showed a faint shade of green.

He looked at Jane, just as she turned to him.

He hated the thought of going downstairs, of guiding her past what they must find.

He dreaded the realization that they owed their lives to deadly creatures probably no less horrible than those who had been destroyed, that his safety and Jane's lay solely in the fact that these deadly creatures did not happen to be informed about them.

Nevertheless, he knew that the road back to their lives was at last clear.

CHAPTER SIXTEEN

Stop Running

WIND RUSHED CLEANSINGLY to either side. Dark trees sped. Overhead the stars fought with the edges of the mushroom of Chicago's smoke. Ahead, Chicago's massed lights glowed pinkish in the air.

Carr and Jane leaned back side by side, holding hands lightly (more than that would not have felt "right" to them this first time), but with their heads close together, so that when they spoke, their voices were masked by the wind and by the old convertible's roar and rattle.

They watched the heads of Tom and Midge in the front seat. They looked at the trees and the stars and the pink of Chicago. It seemed to Carr infinitely strange, yet infinitely natural, that he should once again be a normally functioning part of a vast machine that included the stars and sky and earth and trees and Chicago and Tom and Midge and Jane and himself, a machine that produced planets and people and winds and words. He wondered: "What purpose?" He wondered: "How much consciousness?" Looking at Tom and Midge, he wondered: "Is there truly only darkness inside their minds? Are they only pleasant automatons?"

But those were questions that could not be answered, so long as you stayed part of the machine, so long as you held to the pattern, so long as you did or said nothing that did not seem "right." And he certainly didn't want to be anything but part of the machine now.

"It's been a good first date," Jane whispered to him. "It makes coming back seem a good thing ... even my father and mother, my music, Mayberry. I can almost forget ... many things."

"Better not," Carr reminded her smilingly. "We're not altogether safe, you know."

"But we're back in our lives. They can't notice us— the other 'theys' ."

"If we're careful," Carr persisted.

Jane smiled. "How soon can we get married?"

"When the pattern lets us."

"Suppose it doesn't?"

"It will," Carr assured her.

Jane smiled again. "If it doesn't," she said, "We'll meet outside the pattern."

He squeezed her hand. She looked at him. They were silent for a while. Then, "Why do you suppose it happened to us?" she asked him. "Why should it be you and I that came alive?"

"Who knows?" he said. "Maybe it's like single atoms. They move, they explode, all by chance, no one knowing why."

Jane frowned faintly. After a while she said, "I wonder if we haven't been wrong in some of our guesses. I wonder if perhaps there aren't more awakened people than we realize, living their lives in a trance, sticking to the pattern, but not just because they're nothing but machines, not just because their minds are black. It's so hard to think that Midge and Tom there ..."

"Yes," Carr agreed, remembering something he had momentarily felt at Goldie's Casablanca, "perhaps there are more than we've guessed who are aware, or half aware, who are more than blind machines ..."

"Perhaps," Jane suggested softly, "it's our job to find them, to rouse them fully."

"We'd have to be very careful, sound them out delicately," Carr reminded her.

"Yes. But if we *could* rouse them, if we could make the machine think more and more ..."

"Yes," he said.

"It's so terrible, Carr, to think of those mean little gangs going around—the ones who would have destroyed us, the ones who saved us without knowing—it's terrible to think of them as the only awakened forces in the world ..."

He agreed. "Though we do have at least one ally," she remembered.

"Yes. Old Jules."

For a while they were silent, feeling the rush of the car, watching the darkly gleaming stars keep pace with them.

"I wonder what he was going to tell us," Jane murmured softly.

"He?"

"Fred. The important thing he thought he'd discovered. Do you suppose it was just that—that we should stop running away, that we should try to rouse the half-awakened ones?"

"What knows?" said Carr. But in his heart he knew that he agreed with her, he knew that he could never stay wholly a part of the machine, that he would always be venturing outside its preordained patterns, but on guard now, aware of the dangers, aware of the need to do only the "right" thing much of the time, yet always in search of wakened and half-wakened minds.

The old convertible slowed for an intersection. Midge looked back. Her face was rather impudent, her hair kinky and red.

Carr asked himself: face of a dark-lined machine or of a wakened or half-wakened girl?

Midge asked, "What are you two talking about?" Machine-words or alive ones?

The convertible sped on again.

"Oh," Carr answered, "things." It somehow seemed the right thing to say.

Author's Afterword

OF ALL MY NOVELS, the unluckiest, the most ill-starred and dogged by misfortune was undoubtedly the one I began early in 1943 and ended about ten years later in two quite different versions, the longer *The Sinful Ones* and the shorter *You're All Alone*.

Imagine January 1943. I'd just celebrated Pearl Harbor (the subconscious thrives on death, destruction and dread) by writing my first two novels and they'd just been published in the two pulp magazines edited by John W. Campbell, Jr., *Conjure Wife* in *Unknown* and *Gather, Darkness!* in *Astounding Stories*. Mid-war. As an otherwise unemployed writer, though with wife and small child, I was beginning to worry about being drafted, but I still had that fear well in hand. What's more, my subconscious was boiling up again.

I was fascinated by the idea of a person (or people) who lived in the stacks of a big public library (much as they did in big department stores in John Collier's grand short story "Evening Primrose"). It promised a delightfully melancholy atmosphere, spookiness, all sorts of fantasy devices and endless literary allusions. I thought of combining it with the old philosophical querry of solipsism: "Are other people really alive at all? Are there minds like yours behind the faces?" Which tied in nicely with the question of whether behaviorism was an adequate human psychology: mind described entirely in terms of human action without regard for feeling and thought.

So there I was safely launched on a third novel! I swiftly finished four chapters and as I'd profitably done with my first two books, I sent them off to Campbell in New York City (I was in Santa Monica Canyon, California) for his approval and suggestions.

His reply devastated me. *Unknown,* now *Unknown Worlds,* was ceasing publication because of the paper shortage. He'd be taking no more supernatural stories or novels. And that essentially meant, in the publishing world of those days, there was no market for my new novel anywhere. *Astounding Stories* took only science fiction. *Weird Tales* bought no novels or serials and had been picky about even my shorter offerings. Book publication? —a pulp writer never thought of that, and as a matter of fact, few publishers wanted supernatural tales then, while paperbacks as we know them did not exist.

That was the first bad-luck stroke and probably the shrewdest. If only the news of *Unknown*'s demise had held off for as little as two months! Then I'd have had the book finished and whatever happened then, the material would have been skimmed off my roiling unconscious and that part of me fresh and clean again.

I should have finished the book anyhow, but time and courage had run out on me. I abandoned it and collapsed into a precision inspector's berth at Douglas Aircraft, Santa Monica plant, continuing to write short stories and poetry at a much-reduced rate.

After the war, and still feeling very keenly the literary defeat the war had finally handed me, I got out the four chapters, wondering what to do with them. A fantasy-writer friend read them carefully and agreed with me that hardcover book publication was the best thing to aim for, especially since the situation had improved a little there. William Sloane, whose brilliant supernatural novels *To Walk the Night* and *The Edge of Running Water* had had considerable success, had launched a new publishing house which would favor that *genre*.

So for the next four years, while working full time as associate editor of *Science Digest Magazine* and turning out a few science fiction and horror short stories, writing slowly and carefully I tinkered my third novel into a full 75,000-word existence.

But meanwhile, William Sloane Associates had struck out with Ward Moore's *Greener Than You Think* and Fletcher Pratt's *The Well of the Unicorn* (though both of these novels eventually achieved enviable reputations) and that was the end of their favoring fantasy. I started my own novel on the slow rounds of the other hardcover publishers, enduring rejection after rejection.

My own urge to write more fiction, however, though unstimulated by any more easy successes, was becoming stronger and more imperative all the time. I wrote more and more, engaged my first agent, Frederick Pohl, who suggested I submit the book to Howard Brown and Bill Hamling at *Fantastic Adventures* magazine. I did, and they said they'd take it if I'd cut it to 40,000 words.

I did better than that. In my imagination I went back to 1943, the feelings I'd had then, forget the longer version, and completed *You're All Alone* just as I'd been planning to do it, so far as I could judge, for Campbell and *Unknown*. I was thrilled to see it at last in a magazine.

But that still left the longer version going the slow hardcover rounds. It seemed a pity that so much at-least painstaking work should blush unseen, so when Fred uncovered a possible publisher, I was favorably inclined from the start. Universal Publishers and Distributors were issuing a series of paperback doubles (two novels by different authors bound together) rather like the Ace ones. When they'd heard I had a longer version of *You're All Alone,* they'd pricked up their ears. So off I sent it to them. When they offered me a $500 advance I jumped at it, incidentally signing incautiously a contract without a revision of rights clause.

When it came out in 1953, I discovered that, without consulting me, they'd changed the title to *The Sinful Ones,* inserted a set of more or less sexy chapter titles, and teamed it with a short novel about a lady bull-fighter called *Blood, Bulls, and Passion.* Examining it a little more closely, I found that they'd sexed up two or three of my love scenes in the extremely "soft porn" style and language of the 1950s.

One shouldn't envy the writers who must work in a period of slowly decreasing and liberalizing censorship. Much better, artistically speaking, to turn out books when there's strict and unchanging censorship or none at all. I've been one and I know.

In such transition periods, you see, each writer, if he tries to handle sex at all, is trying to go a little further than he (or the others) did last time, with the result that many "partway" expressions and metaphors are used, ones that only a few years later begin to seem strange, grotesque, even ludicrous.

One of the finest and most moving novels I've ever read is Richard Aldington's *All Men are Enemies,* but turn to the few overt sex scenes (especially the one where the lovers go skinny-dipping) and you'll see how there his language becomes . . . well, I can only say "mighty strange." (One of the best ways of handling it is to make elaborate "fool the censor" jokes of it, as James Branch Cabell did, but that often isn't appropriate in other ways.)

Often it becomes a literally word-by-word battle. When Dashiell Hammett's *The Thin Man* first appeared, the thing I remember people whispering to each other was that it had the word "erection" in it used in its sexual sense. Very oddly, that word no longer appears in new editions of the book, at least the paperback ones. Maybe it sounded too literary to someone, too medical.

Well, anyhow, the contract I'd signed on *The Sinful Ones* had no author's approval for changes clause in it either, so there was nothing I could do about that.

The scene shifts forward about fifteen years to when the paperback publisher, Ace, wanted to bring out the shortish *You're All Alone* as a paperback book, beefed up in length with two of my novelettes, "Four Ghosts in Hamlet" and "The Creature from Cleveland Depths." Perhaps overconscientiously, I thought we ought to have Universal Publishers' permission. They dithered over that for years, although there was never a hint even of reprinting the *Blood, Bulls, and Passion* combo. Eventually I regained rights to *The Sinful Ones* by paying them $500, the exact total I'd got from them in the first place.

Do you wonder that I call my two-head third novel "ill-starred?" Why, even that phrase is too damn good, too poetic, for what happened to that book!

And now *The Sinful Ones* is coming out once more, all by itself this time. I reexamined the book, still more carefully this time. I once had a carbon copy of my original manuscript, but it got lost about seven years ago and I had to work from the paperbook text. I had no copy, for example, of my original love scenes and I was unable to reconstruct them from memory.

I decided, along with my publisher, that the book title and the chapter titles too should stay as they were in the Universal edition. After all, they'd been there for twenty-seven years and they helped identify the book for someone who had seen it in its first form.

In editing the text, I chiefly confined myself to correcting mistakes and confusions that had been introduced during Universal's editings and splicings of the book. And some of those, in all justice, may have been confusions and mistakes in my original manuscript.

But I couldn't leave the sex scenes untouched—they were just too silly and dated, too 1953 soft porn. So I reworked those, writing as I would today, working without the old censorship, yet trying to keep the behavior true to the characters as I'd first conceived them.